JAILHOUSE THERAPIST

MR. RUBILDO

PAGE PUBLISHING, INC.
New York, NY

First originally published by Page Publishing, Inc. 2017

ISBN 978-1-68409-120-1 (Paperback)
ISBN 978-1-68409-121-8 (Digital)

Printed in the United States of America

CHAPTER 1

What would you do if a prisoner standing nearby grabs a razor blade and slashes a person across the face, generating fifty stitches and a puddle of blood large enough to provide a transfusion? I work with the criminally insane, guys who have killed their parents, raped little babies, bank robbers, stickup artists, gangbangers—and 100 percent of these individuals have a substance-abuse pathology. You clearly have to be out of your fucking mind and on drugs to perform such vile acts. Welcome to Rikers Island, where all problems can be solved with a certain degree of violence.

This is an unpredictable world governed by a bizarre set of rules and strange standards. Where normalcy is irrational behavior. When you enter this domain, fear is a constant reminder that you may very well be the next victim in an ever-expanding list of prior prey. No one is above the fray; whether you are a priest, rabbi, corrections officer, or civilian staff member, anyone can be taken down by a raging pack of psychotic lunatics housed on the Rock. Think of a newly born fawn in the savanna of Africa and a pride of lions honing in on its scent. What are the odds of its survival? How I've been able to navigate this hostile environment and remain physically unscathed is beyond my realm of comprehension. My mental status has never been or will it ever be the same since first coming in contact with this unique population.

Emotionally I get drained each time I walk into C-95, the largest penal colony in the United States, housing between 2,500 to 3,500 men at any given time of the year. You automatically begin to make mental preparations on how to remain safe throughout your tour of duty. Despite the fact that I have been working with this population for well over thirty-five years, I still feel somewhat uncomfortable being in direct proximity to them. It's a primal fear programmed into my psyche, which keeps me alert at all times. You become an expert at reading body language, whether someone is posturing with a clenched fist, or did they have bad news during a visit with their girlfriend? Are you in danger? You have to always be vigilant and checking out your surroundings. It's a defense mechanism I have utilized throughout my career in order to survive and keep this overwhelming fear in check.

CHAPTER 2

On May 20, 1973, I began working as a therapist in a group home filled with economically deprived, emotionally disturbed teens ranging from twelve to sixteen years of age. They were a disposable group of children housed in these institutions because nobody wanted them, abandoned by alcoholic or addicted moms who could no longer handle the stress of childrearing. Dads were never in the picture.

They came to us from Spofford, a mini jail for adolescents, a breeding ground for future criminals. If a fourteen-year-old female grew a little breast, adolescent males were relentless in their pursuit to conquer these innocent children. Life for these young women is chaotic. They were never allowed to grow up.

Approximately thirty-five years later while walking in the hallways of Rikers Island, I heard a voice from the past call out to me, "Hey, Mr. Rubildo, you remember me?"

I asked the officer walking this group of men to the medical clinic, "Can I take this gentleman to my office?"

The officer was hesitant. "You know the rules, Mr. Rubildo. I can't do that, they will take a few days from me for breaking protocol. Ask the captain, there she is right behind you." I turned around and saw Captain Green heading in my direction.

She was a difficult person to deal with, always went by the book. Like most officers and supervisors, they didn't want to get caught in a political mess. Letting me bring this guy to my office unescorted could start a firestorm. I asked her, "Capitan Green, can I have a few minutes with this individual in my office? I'll bring him right back."

She was overweight, short, stocky, about four feet eleven inches, with an image problem. It really irked her to provide me with this privilege. "Hurry up and bring him right back when you are finished with him, he has to take his medication," she demanded.

"Methadone?" I asked.

"Don't push me," she said. "It's still his medication."

We were now walking to my office. It would take a few minutes to get there. The hallways at Rikers are hundreds of yards long in either direction.

When we finally got there, I asked Officer Jason, "Can you please open my office?" He was busy and told me, "Take the keys." It was unusual for any officer to hand over the keys. That was their domain; they felt in control. But I've known these officers for over fifteen years, and they trusted me. Other staff members would complain why I was allowed to use the keys. They claim they should be able to open the office themselves. One officer would always tell them, "Next time you spend over thirty years working here, I will personally give you the same privilege."

José entered the office and sat down on a chair in front of my desk and made himself comfortable. I had a bowl full of lollipops sitting on my desk. I asked him, "Would you like one?" He reached over with his trembling right hand and grabbed a cherry-colored one. When he was sixteen years old, he was muscular, athletic, full of energy, and able to dunk a basketball with ease. That was all gone now. It appeared as though he had been in a lot of physical battles and lost many of them.

He had a scar running from near his left temple down to the chin. It looked gross. The change in his appearance was dramatic.

I asked him, "Whatever happened to you?"

He told me, "Soon after leaving Saint Joseph's Children's Services, I began dealing marijuana to support myself. I tried getting a straight job, but I couldn't find one. I moved in with an aunt who lived at the Smith Houses in lower Manhattan, and soon began running with the wrong crowd." He paused for a moment. You could see that the drugs and alcohol abuse had taken a toll on his memory; he didn't appear alert. He was trying real hard not to nod out in front of me. He then continued, "I was told by my boss to deliver a pound of grade A marijuana to the sixth floor at 10 Catherine Slip. As I walked into the building six undercover narcs grabbed me and threw me on the floor. They arrested me and charged me with possession with the intent to distribute, I was fucked big time."

I asked him, "How old were you?"

"I was eighteen," he said, covering his eyes to stop me from seeing that he was about to cry. He went on in detail and said, "When I came out after doing eight months on the Rock, I didn't learn my lesson. Instead I graduated to selling cocaine. The guys inside told me it was more profitable and less risky. You can make deliveries to offices, apartments, you didn't have to hang out in the streets. But while delivering a package, I got busted again. This time I did three years upstate."

"How did you get the scar?" I asked.

"I was twenty-four years old, a baby," he said. "I came home," he continued, "in July 1978—no, '79. It wasn't long before I got arrested again, this time for breaking and entering. I had a real bad heroin problem, shooting between fifteen and twenty bags of dope a day. The judge threw the book at me this time, he gave me four and a half to seven years. If I had gone to trial, I would have to do fifteen years. I took the deal." He had finished licking the lollipop and asked me, "Can I have another?"

I said, "Sure, help yourself." He grabbed a handful and began to put them in his pocket. I gave him a disappointed look.

He said, "I'm sorry! You know how we criminals and addicts are. We can't ever have enough." He put them back in the bowl and took one, green this time. "I was sent to Attica," he said, "where I joined the Crip gang for protection, and they would supply me with drugs. I was high every day while in prison. You just can't survive up there without being part of a gang," he said. "I was just a flunky, a gofer, but if there is trouble you become a soldier for the gang. We got into it with the Bloods. I don't even remember how it happened. All I know is my face was full of blood and I was in a lot of pain."

I asked him, "What would you have done different?"

He said, "Once you get trapped in this type of life, it's difficult to change or be rescued. You'll need an army of people to give you a helping hand in order to get out, it's not easy." He went on to say, "I spent twenty-six out of the last thirty-five years in and out of the joint on drug possession charges, and the time went by in a blink of an eye."

It was as though I was looking at two people. I could still see that young whippersnapper with Olympic athletic ability running around the group home bragging about what he was going to be when he grew up. And this old defeated warrior sitting in front of me barely hanging on to his dignity. The arena that is jail takes no prisoners. You will be defeated one way or another; nobody survives this cruel world without being scarred for life.

I told him, "Let's get out of here, I got to take you back." I walked him over to a corrections officer, and he disappeared at the end of the hallway. I often think about José and why he didn't listen.

CHAPTER 3

I am glad that I am not working at a factory as an innate drone, but that I'm able to be creative and make a difference. Twenty-nine years ago, a young eighteen-year-old teenager came to Bellevue prison ward for the criminally insane under a suicide watch. He had killed a man while under the influence of massive amounts of alcohol and marijuana. Stabbed him to death with a butcher knife he carried for protection.

While there, I walked up to Mr. Jones and asked, "Would you like to talk?"

He gave me a strange glance and said, "Mr. Rubildo, I know these men here respect you, but where I am going, you can't help me. So please leave me the fuck alone."

I asked him in a loud voice, knowing there were staff nearby listening to our conversation, "Is that how you treat adults who are trying to help you?"

This tall lanky African American male with a short Afro was angry at me for calling him out. "I told you to leave me alone, I don't want to talk to anybody," he shouted.

"No!" I told him. "You said to leave you the *fuck* alone. You disrespected me." I was trying to reverse roles by letting him know that I would get indignant if someone disrespected me. And that's just what he had done. He dissed me during this verbal confrontation.

9

In jail and prison, the word *dis* was a biggy. More people have been shot, stabbed, and killed over the word *dis* than you could imagine.

I continued to ask if he wanted to talk, and finally he relented. Pouring out to me all the personal issues cluttering his mind. He said, "I never met my father. He ran out on me before I was even born. My mother placed me in foster care at age four." He was revealing his inner secrets, the pains that led to his self-medication with alcohol and marijuana. He felt abandoned by his immediate family.

He told me, "I quickly began to run away from these group homes. They were just another set of abusive adults trying to stick their dick in my ass."

I asked him, "Are you trying to tell me house parents were involved in this behavior?"

He said, "No one was looking out for children like me. We were sex toys."

I stopped the session abruptly. It felt uncomfortable to continue at this time. We had been talking for nearly an hour, nonstop.

It was early in my career, and I had not been exposed to this type of degradation. When I got home around 10:30 p.m., my mind was still adjusting to the problems this population brought with them. I was unable to sleep. I spent most of the night tossing and turning, looking for relief. I kept looking at the ceiling, and the shadows made me scared. I had a four-month-old baby girl who was going to depend on me forever. I knew there would be other children in our life; my wife wanted a large family.

The next day when we met for a follow-up session, he told me, "When I turned sixteen, I never went back to the group home. I was finished with that part of my life."

I asked him, "Did you become homeless during this time?"

He gave a sarcastic response. "What the fuck do you think? Of course I was homeless."

I was not happy with the way he responded. "Always treat people with respect," I told him. "It doesn't cost anything to be polite."

He told me, "At seventeen, I met a Nubian goddess and got married in a civil ceremony at city hall."

While in Prospect Park and consuming huge amounts of hard liquor and smoking marijuana with five of his buddies, his wife, also an alcoholic, walked into the park. They were newlyweds and still on their honeymoon. One of the guys he was hanging out with said, "That girl has a beautiful ass." He turned to him and plunged a butcher knife into his chest, killing him instantly.

I asked him, "How did you feel after killing him?"

He said, "I had a blackout. All I recall was being arrested a few blocks from Prospect Park, Brooklyn, on Cortelyou Road." He continued to express his anger at being charged with murder. "Now I'm facing fuckin twenty-five years to life, and I don't even remember what happened," he said. "Believe me, I'm not doing no twenty-five years, I rather kill my nigga ass off than to rot in prison," he stated.

"Killing yourself is the punk way of getting out from your responsibility," I told him.

"The judge doesn't want to give me a deal," he said with tears forming in his eyes.

I could see he was still a child with a big problem. "It's not the judge who gives you a deal, it's your defense. You need to work with your lawyer. Use the law library and fight your case with every fiber of your being. Never give up. Then if that doesn't work, you try using your other options. You don't start from the bottom," I told him.

He went to work researching every angle of his case. He was always looking for me to touch base. "Mr. Rubildo," he said, "never give up on me."

I told him, "Never give up on yourself. No one gives a fuck about you. You have to put in the hard work, that's the only way you could succeed."

He was on his way to court one morning when I saw him shackled to other inmates. He yelled out, "Wish me luck, Mr. Rubildo."

He had finally gotten a plea bargain of four and a half to seven years, a far cry from twenty-five years to life that he was originally facing. I wish I could tell you that he did his time and is a productive citizen somewhere in society. But some of these guys can't win with loaded dice. They can't get rid of the demons clouding their judgment.

After doing the rest of his bit, two and a half years at an upstate prison, he returned to the city looking for his wife, who was homeless in the South Bronx. Soon after being dropped off by a corrections bus at Queensboro Plaza, he went straight to the liquor store and bought a fifth of Bacardi rum to celebrate his release from prison. He waited by a hardware store and bought a butcher knife after it opened around 9:00 a.m. The South Bronx, where he was headed, was a dangerous place at the time, and he needed to protect himself.

While wandering aimlessly through the caverns of the South Bronx, looking for his wife, he bumped heads with a friend he knew from the group home and asked him, "Have you seen Sophia?" He told him, "She lives in an abandoned car, two blocks away in an empty parking lot on Chester Street." They spent a few minutes reminiscing the good old days at the group home before he headed to the local liquor store five blocks away on Evergreen Street.

He decided that he needed another fifth of rum to celebrate with his girl. While walking to find her, he gulped down the rest of the bottle he had bought in Queens and was totally inebriated. Eventually he found his wife living in an abandoned car, having sex with a customer she knew well. He used the brand-new knife to kill him. Stabbed him twenty times while his wife screamed hysterically, "Stop! Stop! What are you doing!" He loved her, and by 9:30 p.m. he was back in custody without the possibility of parole.

CHAPTER 4

Some of these cases can be both tragic and comical at the same time, producing outlandish humor and sadness. There was a unique case a number of years ago where an adolescent killed his father, a cat, a blue macaw and decapitated their heads. At the time these macaws were on the endangered species list; they were rare, majestic raptors. One of nature's most profound creations.

When Joey Mohammed arrived at Bellevue Hospital, he was violent and out of control. While Joey was in the holding pen, Dr. Benjamin Levine ordered stat medication. Joey was given Haldol, Ativan, and Cogentin, the standard medication at the time to control violent behavior and schizophrenic pathology. Dr. Levine also ordered that he be held in the intake area for the next hour in order for the medication to take effect, before transferring him to the unit.

Individuals who killed their parents are very scary. They have no regard for human life. But they clearly must have mental problems. It is such an unconscionable act that it leaves the mind numb. Joey had been in and out of mental institution all his life. Since early adolescence he had been diagnosed with paranoid schizophrenia with violent tendencies. He was a time bomb waiting to explode.

The next day I went looking for this guy. I was curious to know why he would kill the bird and decapitate him. It had been over fourteen hours since he had been medicated. I figured he would still be groggy and sedated.

"Mr. Mohammed, how are you doing?" I asked. He was lethargic, drooling, and nonresponsive to verbal commands. I decided to wait another day before I would interview him.

In the meantime, I learned that Mr. Mohammed was an Iranian who was born in the United States. His parents had migrated to our country looking for the American dream. They were persecuted by the Shah of Iran for their political views.

His mother died while giving birth to Joey, and his father never forgave him for losing his dearest love. I guess there was a lot of anger in this household. It seemed that there was a cultural clash between Joey and his father.

Joey loved to smoke crack cocaine, and angel dust. The father wanted him to work and contribute to the household. They disputed about everything.

The blue macaw was given to Joey by an uncle on his mother's side when he was sixteen years old. The father and Joey argued about who would pay to feed this animal. It was a jihad between father and son that never got resolved until he killed and decapitated him.

"Mr. Mohammed, are you feeling better today?" I asked.

"Please call me Joey," he said.

"Okay, that's fine. Do you know why you're here?" I asked him.

"No, I don't know. Could you tell me?" he asked.

"I'll get right back to you," I told him. I needed to clear this with Dr. Levine. I didn't want to overstep my bounds.

I called Dr. Levine and asked, "Can I talk to this guy about what happened?"

He said, "Sure, gather as much information as you can, I would appreciate it. By the way, if he starts to act out, call me immediately."

After hanging up the phone, I went back to the interview room, where Joey sat waiting patiently for me to return. "Mr. Joey, that is what you would like me to call you, right?" I asked.

"It's all right, call me Joey," he said.

"Do you know what you been charged with?" I asked.

"I don't even know why I'm here, but I've been in other institutions like this before," he said.

"You've been in jail before?" I asked.

"No, I've never been in jail before," he said.

"Are you aware that you're in jail now?" I asked, taking a few steps back just in case he lost his cool.

"I'm in jail!" he shouted.

"You've been charged with the murder of your father and lesser charges of animal cruelty. You also have a weapons charge," I told him.

While sitting across from me in a green plastic chair, he slumped over and placed his hands on his face. He stayed silent for a few minutes. I could see he was in shock. "Are you trying to tell me I killed my father?" he asked in disbelief.

"Can you recall any of the events leading up to his murder?" I asked him.

"Not really, all I remember was having an argument with him and smoking a lot of angel dust," he said while attempting to gather his thoughts back together.

The first couple of days is the most difficult period for an individual with mental illness who has committed a murder, especially that of a parent. I asked him, "Are you all right?"

"Yes, I'm okay," he responded in a sad tone of voice.

"I'll come back to see you later," I said.

Joey was standing, leaning against one of the dining room walls, when he waved me over with his hand. "Can we talk?" he asked me.

"Sure, Joey. Anytime you want to discuss something with me, just tell the nursing staff, they'll get in touch with me," I instructed him. "What's on your mind?"

He seemed reluctant at first to talk about it. Finally he said, "I'm beginning to remember what happened."

I asked him, "Would you like to go somewhere private?" We walked out of the dining room and headed to his cell, where no one would disturb us.

"We were sitting in the living room watching television, and he began to yell at me for no reason," he said.

"What was he yelling about?" I asked him.

"Something about me needing to get a job and that I had to stop getting high in his house," he said.

"Did that upset you?" I asked.

"I'm nineteen years old, I want to go to college. I have a lot of time to work in my life," he said.

I was trying to be subtle, not to let him know I was only interested at this time about the bird. "I could understand you being upset with your father, but why did you kill the bird?" I asked.

"That fucking bird was about to snitch on me," he said. This is a schizophrenic patient who thought the bird was about to rat him out. The bird and the cat were the only witnesses to his crime. He was paranoid. He claimed that the bird kept saying, "Joey did it, Joey did it." These patients have a tendency to view reality from a different perspective.

Kevin Smith was a character who always looked devious. He had dreadlocks that ran past the back of his knees, and his rap sheet was a mile long. I first met him when he was eighteen years old. He had an early onset of paranoid schizophrenia.

I was standing by the universal machine, a weightlifting contraption, located in the dayroom, where patients would watch TV

16

and recreate. He was dressed in blue pajamas, Bellevue issued, when I saw him walking toward me. His right hand was palming his ass, and I could tell he was up to no good. When he was a few feet away, he showed me his hand. There were five shit dingle balls in the palm of his hand; they looked like milk duds.

"You ever seen things like this?" he asked me.

I almost lost my composure, but I couldn't let him know that he had gotten to me. So I told him, "I'm not impressed."

"How about this?" he said while popping them into his mouth and chewing away like they were candy.

"I'm still not impressed," even though I felt like throwing up.

"How about this? Will this impress you?" he told me as he took the shit out of his mouth and smeared it on his face.

"You know I'll have to report this incident," I told him.

"Do whatever you have to do, I don't give a fuck!" he said to me, yelling at the top of his lungs.

As I walked to the nursing station to report this incident, I nearly threw up. When I got there, I was pale; the blood had drained from my face. It was so gross that I contemplated quitting.

He was medicated and placed in restraints after made to take a shower. He was screaming and yelling, saying, "I'm going to fucking kill you next time I see you, you're a fucking rat, Rubildo."

Soon he was sedated and out for the count. He later came up to me and apologized.

"I'm sorry for being so crude, I wasn't taking my medication," he said.

"Not a problem," I responded.

He had been cheeking his medication to avoid swallowing it. This is a common practice among psych patients.

CHAPTER 5

After attending thousands of in-services and case conferences and hundreds of lectures over a forty-year career, abandonment appears to be a major component in producing deviant behavioral patterns in male incarcerated individuals. It is estimated that 70 to 80 percent of this population has no father figure or has a dysfunctional parent who was physically and or verbally abusive which has hindered their emotional development.

Sexual molestation plays a big role in creating adverse childhood experiences or early childhood traumas that have a lifelong devastating effect on normal growth.

In this country, we are unwilling to accept this new reality that seven out of ten children ages eight to twelve have been sexually molested by the usual suspects, family members, coaches, priests, or rabbis. There's an endless supply of these predators lurking to pounce on the innocent, and we are turning a blind eye to this new world order. We are launching an unchecked factory of problems that will continue to have unknown ramifications on our daily functions.

Drugs and alcohol are timeless solution to our painful experiences. They've been part of our social fabric for eons. But they don't solve the problems created by our early childhood traumas or adverse childhood experiences. It's understandable drugs and alcohol make you feel good. It disturbs reality, numbs the pain associated with hurtful encounters.

If you review the track record of people who have been drugging and drinking since they were teens, there are five similar components attached to their lives: homelessness, lack of family contact, loss of a job, incarceration, and *they are crazy*.

I've spoken to numerous behavioral health professionals who agree with this concept. Extensive conversations with Dr. Lenny Klein, a forensic psychologist, and longitudinal studies produced by Bellevue Hospital staff seem to confirm this notion that boys without the guidance of a male figure have difficulty attaining success.

Recently, I spoke with Lenny concerning these negative attributes, and he affirmed that there was a definite correlation between abnormal behavioral dynamics and lack of parental supervision.

"We can't be definitive in our conclusion, because of the many variables involved, but it appears that boys have a higher stress level when left to their own accord," he said.

I was curious to know why females are not railroaded into the criminal justice system as readily.

"Women," he said, "have a built-in mechanism that helps in their emotional release. They hug, kiss, and are intimate with each other, part of their nurturing process."

"So are you saying that men don't have the emotional processes that women have?" I asked.

"No, not necessarily, it's just that men have difficulty utilizing this ability to be emotionally attached," he said. He went on to explain, "Sexual molestation plays a big role in creating adverse childhood experiences or early childhood traumas that have a lifelong devastating effect on normal growth." Dr. Klein was reiterating what I had already observed in the past.

Lenny, who looked like he had been eating doughnuts all his life, was at his most comfortable when he was lecturing people. He was capable of rambling on for hours, nonstop; that was his forte. He was the embodiment of an intellectual without an audience, but he made a lot of sense, so I was willing to play the fool for him this time.

His ideas had such a smooth flow to them. It's too bad he was such a condescending prick. He went on to explain how the infiltration of drugs and alcohol has torn apart the social fabric of the nuclear family.

I had to interrupt him, or I would spend the next five hours being lectured without a break.

"Lenny," I said, "I have to go." I made an abrupt exit down the hallway and passed the prison gates. God bless him; that man could talk.

CHAPTER 6

The golden age of forensic medicine started and ended with Dr. Benjamin Levine. I was part of his team. I never intended to stay in this area of medicine for very long. I wanted to make money so I could travel and see the great ruins of the Aztecs, Incas, Mayans, and the pyramids of Giza and walk the Great Wall of China. Instead, I became more intrigued with this notion of the criminal mind. But my money was always short, and I had a growing family with financial demands.

I met an older gentleman who was a disbarred immigration lawyer looking to get back into the game of helping people come to our country. You didn't need to be a lawyer to help an illegal immigrant stay in the country; all you had to do was make marriage arrangements. People would pay him good money for this kind of scam, $5,000. Of course, there were a few minor expenses he would have to cover, but he was walking away with $3,500 after all was said and done. That's how we originally got together in the first place.

I was hanging out in a West Village singles bar on Varick Street, trying to pick up someone I could run into a motel with for a quick sexual encounter. When you're twenty-odd years old, that's all you think about, sex. There's only one thing better than sex, The New York Yankees in first place, in late September.

Aaron was sitting in a dilapidated green-colored booth, ten feet away, with a young Dominican girl wrapped around his arm named Rita Toca. He was staring me down, trying to get my attention. I thought he was homosexual. In the West Village there were a lot of alternative lifestyles that went against mainstream America which attempted to stifle our freedom of expression.

Rita got up and began walking toward me with a cigarette in her hand. "Do you have a light?" she asked. I took a lighter out of my pocket and handed it over to her. "What's wrong with your boyfriend? Why is he staring at me?" I said. "He's a businessman helping single guys make money," she said with a coy smile.

Rita wasn't pretty, but she was voluptuous with big hips, breasts, and a huge round ass. She stood about five feet nine inches tall but had a set of pumps on that were about three inches high. "Is your partner gay?" I asked her. "Certainly not!" she bellowed in indignation.

She walked back to the booth where Aaron sat watching our every move, grabbed him by the hand, and walked him over to me. It was a dance they had rehearsed; they knew the steps well.

She then introduced us like she and I were old friends. "Aaron, this is Mr. Rubildo." We shook hands. He had a good grip, like a man full of confidence.

He began explaining his business proposal in minute details and told me I could make $1,000. I really wasn't interested in his proposition, but I didn't want to let him know how I felt right away. Besides, $1,000 seemed like chump change to make such a commitment as marrying someone I didn't even know. I didn't like the fact that he tried to set me up, using Rita as bait. I figured, somewhere down the road, Aaron would be useful to me. I told him, "I'll think about it and get back to you." He gave me his phone number and said, "Call me anytime."

A few weeks later I got in touch with Aaron and asked if we could do lunch.

CHAPTER 7

Aaron Hirschfield was a debonair, handsome man who exuded class and dignity. Like my father, he wore suspenders and was always dressed to the max.

I needed to make large sums of money. Working at a Staten Island group home and Bellevue Hospital didn't generate enough cash to let me be independent financially. I was always struggling to make ends meet. So I decided to hitch my wagon to Hirschfield and ride his coattail.

Juan, an insurance salesperson who was in cahoots with a crooked attorney named Wilfredo Rivera, told me, "Personal injury cases are the most lucrative part of the legal business." The only problem with this part of law practice is that it takes years before a profit would be made or realized.

I suggested to Aaron that we concentrate our efforts doing personal injury law, which was far more lucrative than immigration law, and he agreed. He opened an office in downtown Manhattan, and we were in business. We used temp lawyers to do our dirty work. I had one nonnegotiable demand: the same day a client was signed, I would get my commission up front. These cases had a tendency to bleed money, and it would take years before they would be profitable. These were shady characters that couldn't be trusted. Personal injury cases take up to three, four, or five years to settle, and who knew where these temp employees would be down the line. In this profession, nearly everyone is corrupt in one way or another. So I had to protect myself from these vultures who had little ethics or no moral conscience.

I quickly began to scour the five boroughs of New York City, including inside Bellevue Hospital, for cases that would produce the cash to propel me to a new financial status. I became one of the best ambulance chasers in New York City. On my first case I made $300. I knew there was a lot more money to come. It was magical.

Kenny Wiseman was the house counsel at our law firm. He was fresh out of law school and dying to make money. He was six feet two, 240 pounds, with curly red hair who was a Jew that looked like an Irishman. He was big, probably capable of playing outside linebacker for a professional football team. He didn't like me, but the feeling was mutual. I never trusted lawyers. There was something about them that rubbed me the wrong way.

Aaron and I sat down to discuss the hiring of a new attorney. We decided it would be in our best interest to hire somebody a little more mature than Kenny. I asked Aaron, "what do you think about getting someone who is retired? An older guy." Aaron was a penny-pincher, always looking for the cheapest way to run our office. You couldn't blame him; he had invested a lot of money to start up this operation. He said, "Hiring someone more mature or a retiree would increase the cost of doing business. Do you really want to do that?" He continued to explain the operation cost. "Right now all we have is immigration law and divorce. We are barely breaking even

One of Kenny's pet peeves about me was that I told him what to do. I would send him to sign up clients for the personal injury business. It would turn his face red whenever I ordered him to do something. And in the middle of this battle was Aaron Hirschfield, who had to make the difficult choices to keep the peace. Aaron had to sit Kenny down and read him the riot act. "Rubildo is in charge, he's the boss, he started this whole thing, this was his idea. So if you cannot handle him telling you what to do, perhaps it is better that you find another place to work."

This infuriated Kenny. "I'm a Yale graduate," he shouted at Aaron. "I can't have this guy telling me what to do."

Aaron told him, "He's a businessman. We're going to let him run the show for now. Everything he's done and said so far has been on the money. I believe in him. So make up your mind. What is it going to be? You either cooperate with him or there's the door, your choice."

He continued to yell at Aaron, with particles of his breakfast flying out of his mouth. "I'm going to stay around for now, but I'm not very happy with this arrangement."

Kenny was never able to see the big picture. He let the fact that I didn't have a degree in law interfere with his judgment. I know Dominican immigrants who came from the backwoods of Santo Domingo unable to read or write, start a business and be successful in this country. They knew that if you buy a dozen bananas for $3 and sell them for twelve bucks, you are going to make a profit of $9.

No doubt Yale and Harvard business schools train individuals to succeed in the capitalist system, but there are other factors that play a role in success, to survive. There is an inherent weakness in the training Yale and Harvard graduates receive. Leadership is a quality that can't be taught. You have to be born with it. You have to be able to tap into people's emotions.

He said, "Using new law school graduates would help maintain the financial cost at a reasonable level. Otherwise, we may have to fold our tents. We can't afford that type of financial hit. A seasoned lawyer would command a large salary. On the other hand, a retiree would not be motivated to wait three to four years down the road to settle a personal injury case. We are in a catch-22 right now. What do you think?"

I said to him, "This is a major acquisition we're making here. We must have someone who can be molded into our thinking." I told him, "I know someone at Bellevue who is both a doctor and a lawyer. Presently he is a nonpracticing attorney. I will talk to him as soon as possible."

Aaron wasn't concerned about who I would bring in. All he worried about was the cost.

The next day I went looking for Alfredo Cancilleri, who worked with me in the forensic unit. He was an early bird, in by six o'clock in the morning, out by one in the afternoon. He ran a private practice out in Queens Boulevard for neurotic psych patients. He was treating a few patients who had been riding elevators during the first World Trade Center terrorist attack. They were suing the city because they were now fearful of riding elevators. He found playing doctor was much more lucrative than being an attorney. His office was always full of Medicaid patients.

He ran a Medicaid mill, handing out prescription narcotics like it was candy. Back in the day the rules and regulations were not as stringent. Today you could not run this type of operation. Doctors were allowed to abuse the system without impunity.

I asked Dr. Cancilleri, "May I have a word with you?"

He said, "Sure, what's up?" I explained to him the nature of our organization. "A friend of mine and myself opened an office in downtown Manhattan, not far off from the Wall Street area."

"What sort of office?" he inquired.

"We hope to turn it into a legal office," I told him. I was aware that this individual had lots of acumen in both the medical and legal field. I had to be careful how I approached him. I would be asking this gentleman to place his license on the line. You never know how someone would react to this sort of request. When I presented my proposal, he told me, "Let me think about it." I walked away from that meeting with him, feeling confident that he would think it over and get back to me.

A few days later he told me, "I think we could do business together. But I'm going to require more details. I want to know everything about what goes on in the office. We will sit down along with your partner and discuss everything."

I told him, "I don't have a problem with that. In fact, I welcome it. We'll put down everything in writing. This way there will be no confusion." I was surprised to learn that many doctors at Bellevue Hospital had both degrees. I don't think it's as prevalent today as it was back then.

There were some growing pains we didn't foresee. The biggest problem we had was whether to have Dr. Cancilleri move his practice into our office downtown. He was adamant about staying out in Queens, where he would be near his home, a few minutes ride from his practice. Traffic in New York City could be murder at any given time of the day. So that was a consideration for him. We had no choice but to acquiesce to all of his terms. And of course I was now in charge of recruiting clients and signing them up.

CHAPTER 8

I was walking on Broadway and Twenty-Eighth Street looking to buy T-shirts, underwear, and socks at a wholesale price. I walked into Mr. Lee's Jewelry Dynasty store, and he said, "This is wholesale only, you need a resale certificate to buy here."

I knew that was bullshit. Show people money and they bite. It is just human nature. I went back the next day with $5,000 and asked him, "Count this for me."

He looked me straight in my eyes and proclaimed, "That's a lot of money, my friend. How can I help you?"

I told him, "I want to know everything about the jewelry business. I want to make money."

He was eager to help me. "First," he asked, "where do you work?"

I told him, "I work at Bellevue Hospital and Rikers Island, but I can't do business at Rikers Island. It is too risky to do business there."

His voice rose several octaves when he stated, "You work at Bellevue Hospital! You have a built-in money-making machine. How many people work there? Do you know?"

I hesitated for a while, trying to gather my thoughts, searching for an answer. I told him, "It's a very big place."

He opened up his eyes wide and said, "I know, I've been there before. There are doctors, nurses, social workers, all kinds of people, you going to do well in that building, trust me."

I told him, "Off the top of my head, five thousand work at Bellevue Hospital."

He said, "Buddha has blessed you. He brought you to me. You and me, we're going to make a lot of money." He advised me, "Never sell to young girls, they can't be trusted. Never sell to guys, they can't be trusted. Never sell to recent hirees, they can't be trusted. Always protect your merchandise, that's your lifeblood." Mr. Lee was a shrewd businessman who would sell his soul to the devil for a dollar. Everything he did was based on making a profit.

I was now in the jewelry business after Mr. Lee set me up with a display case complete with chains, earrings, and bracelets. Only wholesale my ass.

I then proceeded to flood Bellevue with thousands of dollars worth of gold jewelry, and every two weeks, I collected a few bucks. I had thirty to forty people paying me $25 or more each pay period. Along with the money I was making from the law firm, I was beginning to be financially stable. I could go to a bar and spend $60 to $70 and enjoy myself without thinking too much about the consequences. It felt good! But like anything else, if another opportunity comes along, you take the chance.

CHAPTER 9

When Ana Escobar arrived in a 747 jumbo jet in the middle of winter at Kennedy Airport from Medellin, Colombia, without a coat, I felt sorry for her. I had a brand-new leather coat. I gave it to her. She asked me, "Are you sure you want to give me this beautiful leather coat?"

I told her, "Don't worry about anything, just enjoy my gift to you." She began to cry. I asked her, "What's wrong? Are you all right?" But she was unable to control her emotions. She continued to cry her eyes out, and I could never handle seeing a damsel in distress. I was raised by five gorgeous ladies who treated me like a prince. I had to walk away; she was upsetting me. I believe she was experiencing culture shock. Being far away from home for the first time must have been traumatic. But before I could make an exit, she grabbed my arm and asked, "Why are you leaving?"

I told her, "Crying women make me feel uncomfortable."

She assured me that there was nothing wrong. She said, "These are happy tears. Since I got here, everyone has treated me so well, I don't know if I can ever repay them." Before I could utter another word, she hugged me and planted a kiss on my right cheek with her overstated red lips. She said, "Thanks for the coat and for listening."

I said to her, "I thought you were homesick."

"I just got here, of course I'm homesick. I left my mother, father, and children behind. I feel terrible. I don't know when I'll see them again," she said while walking around the room. She continued to verbalize her inner, deepest feelings and stated, "In the last seventy-two hours, my life has changed dramatically. I'm in a strange land with strange people, I'm not sure where I'm going to be tomorrow."

Margarita entered the room. She was the person the drug cartel in Medellin had contacted to make these arrangements. She was to house Ana for a couple of days while the cocaine corporation figured out where she would be most valuable to their organization. It turned out Ana was an airplane mule. She had stuffed twenty cocaine-filled condoms up her rectum and swallowed ten bag of heroin. By now the Medellin cartel was into the heroin business. Margarita and my mother were close friends. She always tried to seduce me with her shenanigans. Margarita was always flirting with the underworld and had connections with cocaine kingpins, but she would never involve me because my mother had given her strict orders not to. She was a crazy bitch who once told me, "I love to rub cocaine on my pussy. It makes me ejaculate all over the place." This short, ugly fifty-five-year-old Mexican tamale asked me, "Would you like to taste my pussy juice?" I was taken aback by her ludicrous remark. "You still have juice in that dry cunt you call a pussy?" I shouted back while I closed the door of her apartment behind me.

Ana never forgot this generous gesture, and a few weeks later she gave me three and a half grams of pure cocaine. I told her, "I do not do drugs." She said, "Sell it, someone will buy it from you." Sure enough there was a market for this drug bigger than I could ever imagine. At first I was leery; being busted for selling drugs is a serious offense. The Rockefeller drug laws were clear and specific.

CHAPTER 10

Margarita was always involved with drug dealers. They weren't your ordinary drug dealers. They were drug cartel bosses, guys who would cut the throat of everybody in your family if you ever double-crossed them.

One day while I was staying with Margarita, I told her, "A guy by the name of Pablo called." She replied defensively, "What did you tell him?" I said to her, "Nothing, I just told him you weren't home."

Margarita was always nervous, edgy, but today her main concern was Ana. "I don't want you getting involved with that girl," she said. "Stay away from her."

I responded to her with a stern warning by saying, "I'm a twenty-nine-year-old man, I do what I want."

She insisted, "Just stay away from her, she's very dangerous, you could get hurt." It mattered little that Ana was standing in the room while this dispute between us was going on. Ana didn't speak any English. "You with your curly hair and good looks," she said. "You could have anybody. Why are you gonna mess with this girl?"

I told her, "I never had a Colombian girl."

She was furious. She said, "Get out my house."

"Okay, you win, I'll leave her alone," I responded.

I was on my way out of the apartment when Ana ran up and thanked me again for the coat. "Thank you very much for the coat, I really appreciate it," she said.

I told her, "You're welcome." And I walked out.

My mother gave Margarita strict orders not to get me involved in the drug trade. Margarita was a free spirit who didn't give a fuck about anything, and if given the opportunity, she would get me started in a drug career.

When I was seventeen years old and trying to get away from my parents due to their constant harassment, Margarita took me in for a few weeks. She had been part of my life for a long time, my mother's best friend.

My mother went up to Margarita. She was infuriated that she had taken me into her place. It would undermine her authority. "Are you crazy?" she said. "That's my youngest son, are you going to corrupt him with your crap? Emerito, his father, is going to kill you, believe that," she said.

She yelled back at my mother, "Teresa, relax." Margarita was trying to deescalate the situation, which was getting out of control. She asked my mother, "What would you have me do, let him be out in the streets homeless or take him in? Your choice." Margarita was standing with her arms on her hips in defiance. By this time my mother was in better control of her anger.

Margarita always seemed to be more logical than my mother. She was less emotional in her decision making.

In the late 1940s, Margarita was told by a big white guy to get up from her subway seat so he could sit down. She refused. She was a proud Mayan Indian, with dark skin, who stood up against a racist establishment and won. There are numerous individuals who would never be given the credit for standing up against social injustice. But Margarita, she's my hero, and that's not a sandwich I'm talking about.

CHAPTER 11

A guy I knew once told me, "Get seven to ten cocaine customers with money and never ever give credit. Make sure you have the money in your hands before that customer walks away from you, or else you'll kiss that coke cash good-bye. Trust me, don't trust anybody when it comes to dealing drugs. If you're taking the chance, then you have to be sure to get paid in full right then and there, not next week."

I was still not sure what to do with this newly found connection, whether to embrace it or leave it alone. The demons got the best of me. How would I go about developing this new potential treasure? In the back of my mind I had a consuming fear of the unknown, the possibility that I would be dragged into court in handcuffs. Plus, I was morally conflicted.

The next time I saw Ana, she gave me her beeper number and told me, "Call me anytime." Margarita, the old mother hen, was cock-blocking, and I was unable to talk to Ana. Before I left, I signaled to her with my hand up in my ear. I told her, "I'll beep you right away." The drug cartel bosses had rented an apartment for her at Ninety-Second Street, between Twenty-Third and Twenty-Fourth Avenue in East Elmhurst, Queens, a fifteen-minute drive from where I lived. The neighborhood was beautiful with tree-lined streets and mainly attached homes, a quiet area. Apparently, she had been ordered to set up shop there and wait for further instructions. It appeared Ana was well connected, a captain in this business.

While running up the stairs to her stoop, I saw her peek out the window. She had been waiting for me to show up. She opened the door decked out in a seductive dress exposing her voluptuous breasts and in a shy voice said, "*Hola*, Marcelo. I'm happy to see you again, come in."

I said, "I'm glad to be here, thanks for inviting me."

The apartment had been hooked up, new furniture, stereo, and a telephone. "This is your place?" I asked in shock at the opulence that was given to her in such a short period of time.

"Yes, this is all mine, for now," she said.

"I'm very impressed," I told her. "How did you manage to do this so quickly?"

"We'll talk about that later," she said. "Right now I want to sit down and have a talk. I need you to teach me how to drive, how to get around the city," she said.

"That's why you brought me down here, to ask me to teach you how to drive?" I asked in a loud voice.

"What were you expecting, a quick piece of ass?" she said.

"You want me to be honest? Yes, I was expecting to get a quick piece of ass."

"I'm a lady! I have to be in a relationship before I even think about letting a man touch me." She was incredulous that I had come here with the intent to get fucked. "I just met you a few weeks ago, why don't you give it just a little time?" she said. "I'm not an American girl. Where I come from, we have morals."

We began to get close, but I was also able to see a darker side of her. A part of her that she tried hard to hide with her flirtatiousness and humor. But I was able to see her bossiness and moodiness whenever she didn't get her way. I had been reading body language for well over a decade when I first met her. I knew that there was something sinister about her. No one gets a furnished apartment without having to pay a price. Finally I asked, "How are you paying for this apartment?"

"Do yourself a favor and stay out of my business," she said in a stern tone of voice that threw me aback with its harsh wording.

"Either tell me what's going on in your life or I walk," I shot back.

"Okay, you want to know what I do?" she screamed at the top of her lungs. "I've been sent here by the Medellin drug cartel to establish a wholesale drug ring," she said. "I didn't want to get you involved. This is a dangerous business, and I will not be able to protect you if something goes wrong. These are bad hombres who will hold your whole family hostage to get what they want. Please stay away, I beg you."

I wasn't impressed with her plea. I told her, "I can take care of myself."

She said, "You have no idea what you are getting into. These people are ruthless, they will kill your whole family."

"Let me worry about that," I told her. "Just show me the business and tell me everything about it, I could handle it."

The following Saturday I took Ana out to Jones Beach, Long Island, at six o'clock in the morning, when the large parking lot was empty. I told her, "Drive around until you get tired." I warned her not to go around the edges of the parking lot. "Stay in the middle." This went on for several weeks as she began to feel comfortable with the car. By now she had gotten her driver's permit and was able to drive on the city roads with somebody who had a license.

The next day, early in the morning, I beeped her to a Bellevue phone. She responded to my call right away. I said, "Hello."

"It's me Ana. How are you doing?" she asked me in a soft, tender voice.

"I'm okay, how can I help you?"

"Well, now that I have my own place, I wanted to know if you would like to stop by for a minute."

"You sure you would like me to stop by?" I asked in a devious tone of voice.

"Sure," she said. "Do you remember my address?" I wrote it down on a napkin and told her I would be there by four thirty this evening. She said, "Okay, I'll be waiting for you," and hung up the phone.

I was excited with the anticipation of meeting up with her later that evening. The day dragged by working at Bellevue. I had called out sick at Rikers Island as part of my plan to seduce Ana. I stopped off at the liquor store to buy a flask of wine, hoping it would put her in the mood for lovemaking.

Ana explained, "Once I'm settled in, I will call for my family and have them move here. I have connections in Columbia who would be supplying me with material that I have to sell. In return my connections will help me get my family over here." She continued to elaborate on this scheme engineered by her boss. "I have three young daughters and a twelve-year-old son. My husband and I are separated, but for the purpose of this business, we will act like we're still husband and wife." She continued to break down the design of her business. "I can't have any interference, like a relationship."

I asked her, "What about me?"

She was emphatic in her reply. "No relationships. If you like, I'll help you make money. You will get rich with my supply."

I was wasting my time. I decided, "I'm going to take you up on your offer to make money. It has always been one of my favorite hobbies," I said to her.

She was right. Her cocaine was so good, 97 percent pure, that you can stomp on it three times and quadruple your money. But I wasn't greedy. I kept my material potent in order to entice my customers, to keep them coming back.

I had Ana's beeper smoking, ordering two, three times per week for a few ounces of white powder that was now turning into gold.

I felt disappointed that she did not accept my sexual advances, but I finally let it go.

CHAPTER 12

When I made a concerted effort to get involved in the cocaine trade, psychiatrists became my biggest customers. I guess they felt connected somehow with Sigmund Freud, who is considered the father of psychiatry. Whatever the reason, they took to cocaine real hard, fascinated by its effect. The reality is that they got caught up in a disease that destroyed every one of them within a short period of time. Few people can handle this powerful narcotic and walk away unscathed by its emotional effect. There are doctors that once they finish operating on a patient run to their office and snort a couple of lines of the powder. In the past, employees would have three martinis with their lunch; today it is three lines in each nostril. You'll be surprised at how rampant and entrenched this activity is in our society. It's on Wall Street, the local bars, and lawyers do it too. There's not one segment of our society that's not getting high on this drug. Piss test any profession, and the drugs of choice found in their system will be marijuana and cocaine. It's not just in the ghetto; it's everywhere. When I was growing up, drug use was considered counterculture; today it's mainstream.

Bellevue Hospital attracts the most gifted geniuses known to man. Forensic psychiatrists had a fabulous mental acuity for understanding the criminal element; they were in the forefront of this realm of medicine, a magnet for research in this ever-expanding esoteric field, the Mecca of forensic science. Their adroit techniques and skills were masterful in their versatility. Bellevue's administration gave us the freedom to perform scientific experimentation that bordered on the unethical, but at the same time innovative. Who would question the integrity of these doctors? They were beyond reproach.

And when it came to partying, these doctors took it to the highest level of pleasure-seeking behavior, and cocaine became overnight their drug of choice. They had an amazing stamina for this recreational drug, getting high both day and night. It was a nonstop frenzy, and it's difficult to describe to your average layperson how these doctors went fanatical for this drug. I was on constant speed dial to service these individuals. If I couldn't get to them, they would drive anywhere in the city to pick up their stash.

I went to Dorney Water Park in Pennsylvania for a week of rest and relaxation with my children. I had brought along seven grams of pure cocaine, light pink, fish scale, for my own personal use. I got a call from Dr. Richard asking me for an eight ball of cocaine.

"Are you busy right now?" he asked.

"Dr. Richard, I'm on vacation," I told him.

"I'm willing to drive anywhere to see you," he said.

"Right now I'm in Pennsylvania, at a water theme park, close to one hundred miles away," I said with an incredulous attitude.

He said, "That's not a problem, tell me where you are and I'll get there within a few hours."

I didn't even like this doctor, and I resented his pressuring me to help him out with his addiction.

"I don't want you to interfere with my vacation time," I told him.

"It'll take two minutes of your time, honestly," he told me. "Where are you?"

I gave him the address, and within a few hours a black stretch limousine was parked in front of the motel room where I was staying with my family. He had a courier drive nearly one hundred miles to pick up his shit. I charged him $100 extra for my inconvenience.

This is why cocaine is known as the drug of the rich. These doctors had huge amounts of expendable income to party, with no visible consequences for their action.

Poor Anita, a fellow co-worker was left to raise a family of four by herself with less than $40,000 in income per year. Where is the justice?

While waiting for this motherfucker to get in touch with me, he called. His intrusiveness was unbelievable. He wanted more coke.

"Do you have anything else besides this eight ball?" he asked.

Dr. Richard didn't think twice about spending well over $4,000 to get his fix, one-tenth of Anita's salary for the year, before taxes.

Before September 11, 2001, the Wall Street area was awash in marijuana and cocaine used by nearly everyone who worked there. Bellevue Hospital was no different. If ever they tested the staff, half of them would have to be discharged for illegal drug usage.

The bombing of the World Trade Center changed the way business was conducted in the entire Wall Street area. Security became so tight it was nearly impossible to conduct any kind of transactions. Before 9/11, you could walk into these buildings without any difficulty, but now you need a slew of credentials to enter the Merrill Lynch building or the Hanover tower. Homeland Security became paramount in how security was conducted in the financial capital of the world. You don't develop this type of clientele by going up to them and offering to sell a gram of coke. You have to be super cautious, gather information, read body language before you could make a move.

I've heard that Dr. Friedman, since he was an intern, was reckless and a user. He had a box of tissues in his office and was always blowing his nose, a clear sign that he used an inferior product. If you cut cocaine with lactose, that's the adverse reaction you have, a constant dripping nose. He also grew his pinky nail about three quarters of an inch long, another telltale clue of his use.

He also smoked two packs of Camel nonfiltered cigarettes a day and was always irritable. I knew he had a jones, a slang term for addiction.

I finally formulated a plan and decided to ask him point-blank whether he would like to use my product.

"Dr. Friedman, may I have a few words with you?" I asked.

"Sure, Mr. Rubildo, what's on your mind?" he said.

"I would like you to know we have the strictest confidentiality privilege between us," I told him. "If I offend you in anyway, then this conversation is over."

My heart was beating out of control. I had sweaty palms and armpits with a malodorous stench. I felt like I would pass out any minute from the pressure I placed on myself with this pending request.

"Rubildo, I know where you are coming from, you don't have to stress yourself out," he said.

Within a few minutes I was able to relax. The pressure was off. I knew right then and there he was my customer for life. We ignited a friendship that is still going strong today.

Over the next eighteen years he spent well over $500,000 buying this drug from me. He was never free of its influence, but despite being high every day, he still had good judgment at the workplace, which is rare.

Unfortunately for him, his upper cartilage palate became so decayed it needed to be replaced with a metal prosthesis. He also had a perforated septum, which compromised his nasal structure. No medical procedure would be able to repair this advanced damage.

This was the result of decades of abusing hydrochloride topical, the acid found in cocaine. Nothing would deter Dr. Friedman from using cocaine. Even after having his palate reconstructed, he continued to indulge himself with this drug.

CHAPTER 13

I was the new Jack on the unit, and everyone was still trying to figure me out. They were the intellectual Harvard graduates in a specialized field, but they didn't have the street savvy I brought to the plate.

I presented a conundrum to them. They felt I shouldn't be here. When you're surrounded by white Anglo-Saxon Protestants and Jews who have been in the forefront of this type of medicine, they want to know why you're there.

They were in the process of experimenting with neuroleptic medications, and black men would be their guinea pigs. Medications like Zyprexa, Abilify, and Neurontin were part of the pharmaceutical companies' attempt to make money. The health-care profession has ballooned into a $400 billion conglomerate, a money tree waiting to get plucked by unscrupulous doctors.

Many of these psychiatrists were in cahoots with the pharmaceutical companies. They would wine and dine them and give them extravagant gifts. One of these psychiatrists was given a $400 pen by a pharmaceutical representative, and he had the audacity to go around showing it off to his colleagues as though it was a trophy.

They had no moral principles. It mattered little to these doctors that they would be exploiting the most vulnerable individuals, people who have no support systems available to them, and America wonders why black men are so angry with the establishment. There's a potential, explosive rage lurking within the confines of jail and prison that's about to manifest into a racial war.

If you listen closely to these patients, you hear a similar repertoire being regurgitated about the theme of this secret cabal. I've spoken to hundreds of men concerning this complicity, not only in jail, but across the social spectrum. And many feel there is a synchronized social injustice taking place across the country. Social workers, doctors, therapists, men of color repeat verbatim similar concepts that echo throughout the jail and prison system. They feel like expendable commodities to be exploited by the established powers, an attempt at enslaving their mental prowess.

Hitler's tyrannical Germany produced a satanic culture that nearly exterminated the Jewish nation because they felt Aryans were superior humans. Their intent of world domination is a misnomer. Everybody hates the guy on top.

When I first started working at Bellevue Hospital, I hated my boss. I wanted to undermine everything that he wanted to do. He didn't want me there. I was a threat to his authority. A new Jack is never welcomed. I made them feel uncomfortable with my presence. I had traversed into their domain, basically unannounced, and they wondered if I was a spy.

They had no idea I didn't give a fuck about their ritualistic morass. All I wanted to do was sell cocaine, get personal injury cases, and peddle my gold jewelry.

I had traveled a long way to achieve my personal goals, and these morons were just stepping-stones. I knew that I was part of this affirmative action program to make a level playing field so that we can compete with other races. In reality, they had to lower the standards so people of color could get into the mix.

Let's remove this barrier of affirmative action so we can achieve greatness.

Men of color have been habituated to think defensively whenever confronted by police, because they're not viewed as law-abiding citizens.

There is a concern because these men don't support the nuclear family unit, and their children can be easily victimized. Promiscuous activity is paramount on their agenda. The macho image must be preserved at all cost according to misguided cultural values. Young men of color are being spoon-fed a ridiculous dream, which very few could achieve, that being a rapper or professional ballplayer is the ultimate goal. It's a perverted ideology that leaves them vulnerable to abuse. These ambitions are not educationally based. Gifted athletes are often pampered throughout their high school and college careers with little emphasis on education, and rappers don't even need to graduate from high school to have a successful vocation.

A coach I had in high school told me, "Rubildo, you're a decent athlete, but you're never going to get to the pro level, you would be wise to get yourself a good education."

He crushed my spirit. I always thought of becoming a major league baseball player. Here was a man I looked up to as a father figure telling me I wasn't good enough to make it in the pros, my life dream.

I was so angry I wanted to beat the crap out of him. Deep in my heart I knew he was right. He only had my best interest in mind. This tough love he provided redirected my thinking, and I knew I had to make a bigger effort at getting my education instead of amusing myself with a dream that would never materialize. James Glenn continues to be my hero to this day for giving me a heads-up on reality.

How many African American or Latino males have someone like that looking out for them? Glenn's spiritual intuition continues to reverberate through my conscience development, and I would thank him if I could for giving me this insight.

CHAPTER 14

I was now in a good groove, and cash was flowing in from multiple directions. I needed to diversify this income from drugs, gold jewelry, and the law firm. What was the next stage of my nefarious activities? I again flooded the great institution of Bellevue with another thing they needed, cash.

I began lending money to anybody who was desperate, and I believe half of this institution falls under this category.

There were so many people looking for loans I feared my cash flow would be exhausted. But soon the market stabilized, and I was rolling in dough. I would lend $1,000 for a $300 vig commission. My clients would pay me a minimum payment of $100 per pay period. It would have been harder for me to print money. Bellevue morphed into a cash cow overnight.

I had a chifforobe in the basement of my house stacked with bundles of hundred-dollar bills collecting dust. The money was worthless since it couldn't be spent without arousing the curiosity of the IRS. I feared the government would confiscate my hard-earned cash.

I invited Carmine Bono, a shady bank president who ran a Chase Manhattan branch on Fourteenth Street and First Avenue, to my house for dinner. I wasn't 100 percent sure, but I think Carmine was mob connected. I met him at a house party in Bensonhurst,

Brooklyn, and he was surrounded by a bunch of Italians with odd nicknames. He was dressed in an Italian knit with silk pants and pointy black shoes; he was a snappy dresser. He could have easily been a supermodel with his tall, slender build and chiseled features. He looked like a Roman god. That night, he gave me his business card and I asked him for a few tips on financial planning. A few weeks later I invited him to my home for a meal of rice and beans with *pollo frito*, I asked him, "Come downstairs with me."

We finally stood in front of the wardrobe. I swung the doors open, and a pile of cash lay sprawled at the bottom. He didn't appear shocked. As a matter of fact, he looked nonchalant. As though this was commonplace occurrence for him.

"How much you got there?" he asked.

"A few hundred thousand," I told him.

"You don't have an exact number?" he said in dismay.

"I really don't have the time to sit around and count it all," I explained to him.

He seemed a little irritated that I was running this business off the cuff without books or protecting my finances.

"The first rule of business," he said, "you keep track of every penny you earn." He continued to verbally castigate me for running a business so frivolously. "This is your lifeblood," he said. "You must protect it."

We went back upstairs, and he informed me, "I'm going home to get a money counter, I should be back within an hour."

He jumped into his brand-new Cadillac and sped off like a bat out of hell. I was stunned but glad that he was going to give me a hand to manage my money.

He was at my door with the money counter in a little over an hour. We headed straight to the basement. He was excited.

"I will have to move this money out of the country, it's getting really difficult to launder money nowadays," he said.

I asked him, "What is this all going to cost me?"

He was taking the money counter out of a nice black leather bag when he turned to me and said, "Traditionally it's 20 percent, but since you know Salvatore, I'll clean your money for 15 percent."

I said, "That's a lot of money."

Salvatore was the guy that threw the party where I met him. You could tell he was a made man. His daughter Nicole had invited me to this festivity. She wanted to know me better. But once I saw her father, my interest waned. Guys like this could make your life a living hell. I had a similar problem with Giovanni Serpentine, the father of Anita, the prettiest and richest girl in the town of Warwick, New York.

I could hear Salvatore in my head warning me, "Don't fuck with my daughter!"

Carmine was getting a little upset. I had just met him, and I could tell he had a short fuse. "I tell you what," he said. "Shop around, and if you can get a better price than 15 percent, take it." I wasn't going to back down. We were negotiating.

"No," I said, "you give me a better price."

He said, "What do you think is a good price?" I didn't want to sound or appear ridiculous. This was the president of a Chase Manhattan bank who knew his business. I didn't want to offend him by making an outlandish demand where he would be spooked. I need this guy to help me.

Finally I suggested, "Between 10 and 15 percent would seal it." We were standing inches away from each other. I could smell the beans, rice, and pollo frito on his breath.

"Thirteen percent is the best I could do," he said.

"I could live with that," I quickly replied.

I was feeling good that I had beaten this banker at his own game. We sat down to count the money, and he was strictly business. We barely spoke. I removed the money and placed it in front of him while he inserted wads of cash into the machine. That contraption was running nonstop for forty-five minutes when I turned to him and asked, "Would you like a beer?"

He said, "Do you have any liquor?"

I told him, "I have rum and whiskey, let's take a break." The meter on the machine was sitting at $185,350, and we weren't even halfway through counting.

We made our way into the kitchen, where I asked him, "What's your poison?" He sat on one of the stools surrounding my peninsula countertop and said, "Give me whiskey on the rocks." After pouring him a double shot of J&B whiskey over ice in a medium-size glass, I asked him, "What's your plan?"

He placed his elbows on top of the black pearl granite countertop, and while sipping his drink, he said, "I'll have to move this money to an offshore account somewhere in the Cayman Islands. I know some people down there, they'll help us out." He went on and asked, "What do you plan to do with this money? You have probably over $500,000 sitting downstairs."

I was not sure what I wanted to do with this cash. All I knew was that I couldn't leave it sitting downstairs. I told him, "My first preference would be to leave it for my kids."

His eyes lit up when I mentioned that I wanted to leave it for my kids. He said, "Listen, I'm a family man, and I'm always looking for ways to leave a nice inheritance for my children, that's a good investment. But what about your present needs? What is it that you want to do now?"

He was beginning to expose himself to me, showing a more endearing quality to his character. Alcohol has a tendency to lower people's defenses. Give them a few drinks and they pour their hearts out to anyone who would listen. I told him, "I don't see my business slowing down anytime soon, so financially I'm okay."

He looked surprised and asked me, "Are you trying to tell me you accumulated this type of wealth and there's more to come?"

I knew he was about to ask me about my personal business, how I got the money. I learned a long time ago not to trust anybody. But this was my personal banker. How was I to respond?

I poured him another double shot of whiskey, and he was beginning to be a little tipsy. He seemed more interested now in my personal life than the cash sitting downstairs. I didn't want this individual to be my friend. I just wanted him to take care of my problem.

He asked, "Do you expect this cash flow to continue?"

I said to him, "Why don't we go back downstairs and finish counting the money." He got up, stretched himself out, and nearly fell. He was drunk.

He could hardly walk down the stairs, but he insisted that we finish counting the money tonight. I was trying to hold up this 210-pound individual who weighed nearly 30 pounds more than me, and I couldn't do it. I let him drop gently to the floor. "Carmine, what the fuck is wrong with you?" I asked him.

"I'm not feeling well," he said.

"Why don't we leave this for another time, the money is not going anywhere?" I said.

"Rubildo, we need to get this done tonight," he said in a slurred speech.

He was unable to sit or stand, so I laid him down on the futon I had down in my basement. His body was too big; part of his legs dangled past the armrest. He looked like a clown. This guy had a low tolerance for alcohol.

Saturday morning he woke up with a splitting headache and disorientated. "Where the fuck am I?" he yelled at the top of his lungs.

I rushed down to greet him before he could get out of hand. "Hey, calm down," I told him. "I have two young girls in here, they can't see you like this."

He was a pitiful figure sitting there not knowing where he was staying.

"Give me a few minutes," he said, "to get my head back together again."

I told him, "Take your time. You are not working today, are you?"

He was still in a fog and needed an aspirin to calm down his aching head. "No," he said while stumbling out of the futon and onto his feet. "But I would like to finish taking care of your money."

I told him, "Leave that for another day, we can get back to it. The money is not going to go away. Why don't you go home, take a shower, and relax."

He said, "That whiskey really kicked my ass last night, but you're right, we'll get back to it."

I asked him, "Would you like to wash up? I have an extra toothbrush."

He said, "Yes, if you don't mind."

I took him to the first-floor bathroom and gave him a new toothbrush and a tube of toothpaste. There was already a bar of soap sitting on the sink. He cleaned himself up and just before leaving said, "I'll call you sometime during the week." He then jumped into his red Caddie and made a right on 160th Street, heading toward the highway. He was going to take the Whitestone Bridge to where he lived in the Bronx, Parkchester Road.

He called me on Thursday wanting to get together Saturday evening. I told him, "I get home by seven o'clock."

We finally completed counting the money. The tally was $490,350. To this day, I'm still getting monthly statements confirming the money was transferred to the Cayman Islands.

But I became spiritually empty. The money felt dirty. I began to abuse it. I knew that I had taken advantage of everyone around me.

CHAPTER 15

Dr. Cancilleri called a meeting for tomorrow afternoon at his Queens office. Aaron, who lived in Manhattan, took a cab. I drove there and parked a few blocks away. I hated to pay meters or parking garages; it went against my grain.

Dr. Cancilleri's office was opulent. He sat on a large dark green leather swivel chair behind an immense oak desk that occupied half of the space in the room. Just as we sat down, his secretary brought us coffee and doughnuts. I wasn't really into drinking coffee. It made me edgy; the kick reminded me of cocaine.

"I have major concerns about our legal caseload," he said. "Ninety-seven percent originates from Bellevue Hospital, this is a red flag."

I never even thought about this discrepancy. It made sense to me. It would attract too many eyes to our practice. The feel-good doctor was meticulous about how he did business. He had an impeccable acuity for detail. Those Harvard graduates were well trained.

"What would you propose we do?" I asked him.

"We only have two options at this time," he said. "We can farm them out or sell them outright."

I asked him, "What is the best thing we could do financially?"

He looked somewhat puzzled, trying to make the best financial decision for our firm. I knew right then and there that he had our best interest in mind.

"You have to understand that if we farm these cases out from Bellevue, it's going to take years before you see a return," he said. "But if you sell them, you'll have cash to run your business."

I told him, "Not for nothing, but I thought this was our business."

He responded, "Where are you going to be five years from now?" He was giving me the financial reality of this business, and Aaron sat there not saying a word. He didn't want to get involved in arguments between partners. He was a shrewd individual who had paid his dues a long time ago. It seemed as though he was doing this just for fun.

"Aaron, what do you want to do?" I asked him, just to get him involved in the conversation.

"I never practice personal injury law, I was always involved with immigration. So I really don't know what to tell you," he said.

"I'll be honest with you," Dr. Cancilleri said. "Don't depend on me to be here five years from now. I'm going to stay as long as possible, but things could change tomorrow."

I could see that he had no loyalty to our firm, a freelancer. If a better deal came along, he would take it; that's what he said. That's why degrees are so important. If you don't have one, then you have to depend on these asshole to help you or, should I say, help themselves.

This legal whore that processed our cases wanted to pass me around like a bitch, because of fear that too many of these cases came under the Bellevue Hospital umbrella. He didn't want to continue receiving all these cases, so he created an elaborate scheme to cover our tracks.

The new group that became a mainstay in our business would wine and dine me at the most exclusive restaurants in New York City.

Money was no object to them. They gave me carte blanche to order whatever I wanted. At one place I ordered a $1,500 bottle of wine just because I could and knew there would be no complaints from the group that was trying to fuck me with their shenanigans. When you're making hundreds of thousands of dollars for these guys, they go all out for you.

CHAPTER 16

During this period in my life, I met Julio Diaz while I was attending paralegal school on Forty-First Street, between Broadway and Sixth Avenue, in midtown Manhattan. We quickly became inseparable friends. It also helped that he worked in the legal department at the MTA. If you got run over by a subway or bus, he would be privy to all the information. He too was trying to supplement his income.

Diaz was a dark-skinned Puerto Rican who wore designer clothes and was the epitome of coolness.

One night on our way back to Queens we stopped off for drinks. We went to a strip joint on Northern Boulevard called Honey. I always preferred to have my drinks poured by a half-naked blonde than a burly bartender.

It was early in our friendship, and I didn't know much about Diaz other than that he worked at the MTA. He wasn't a very talkative guy, but when he said something, it was usually profound.

I asked him, "What are you planning to do with your paralegal certificate once you graduate?"

He said, "I'm not sure yet. I just know I have to get out of the MTA. I've been working there for twelve years, that's long enough."

I asked him, "What is it you do there anyway?"

He said, "I'm an insurance claim adjuster. Whenever the MTA gets sued, I try to figure what's the best remedy."

I became intrigued. Anytime the words *sue* and *insurance* come into play in a conversation, you know that there's a payoff somewhere down the line. I needed to know more about what he did at the MTA without letting him know my ulterior motives. I was trying to gain his confidence.

"So you're in the forefront of the MTA's insurance department," I asked.

"You could say that," he responded. "Why are you so interested?" His mood seemed to change, and I felt a little defensive now.

"No reason, just a little curious," I told him.

"I know exactly what you are thinking. If you can get a lawyer to work these cases, I have an unlimited supply of them available for you," he said.

"I have a network that will take care of all of these problems," I told him.

By now I had a few lawyers working on our cases. I was even able to pluck a couple of criminal cases out of Bellevue Hospital prison ward.

Then there was the question of residual cases. If a client signed up with us, it was likely that these cases could generate additional business. If a family member of a signed client needed legal advice, they would utilize our firm or use the lawyers we had farmed some of our work to. We couldn't trust these additional lawyers to do the right thing by us; they would keep these cases for themselves. This was common practice among these lawyers. It was a hidden treasure trove.

Diaz jumped at the opportunity to make money by selling his MTA cases. "If it's true that you have a solid foundation to work these cases, then I'm in," he said.

It didn't take much to convince him to join our team of ambulance chasers.

"I even have a secretary named Loretta working in the x-ray department looking for cases, and I'm going to tell you what I told her. I don't want any cases from Jews or Caucasians, only Latinos and African Americans. Jews and Caucasians know the law. They could get us in trouble, we always have to cover our ass," I told him.

We made millions for these lawyers, and what we got in return was peanuts in comparison. But these greedy fucks were never happy. They could never get enough cash in their coffers. Now Diaz became a focal point in their devious plan. His contribution would change how they distributed the money. Diaz also wanted his money up front.

With these MTA cases, the payouts were astronomical. If you fall onto a subway track and a train runs you over, severing one or more of your limbs, it could generate a half million to a million dollars easily. Therefore, our commission had to dramatically increase in size.

Diaz asked for $1,000 per case, which I thought was cheap, so I in turn added another $1,000 to boot. I always had to get mine. Remember, these motherfuckers couldn't be trusted to do the right thing by you, so I had to squeeze the orange now. In fact, it's been well over a decade since I was forced to resign from the personal injury business due in large part to an ongoing criminal investigation by then New York City attorney general, Robert Weinstein. Not one of these scumbags ever called me again. So I was wise to get my money up front. Like I always said, you don't have to wait for judgment day. Everybody gets paid in full right here.

Diaz became a workaholic, bringing one to two cases per week, and he told us he could deliver even more if necessary. We are talking about $200,000 to $300,000 in commission between him and me. These cases were vigorously challenged by the city. They do not hand over the money without a fight. On the average it takes nearly seven years to settle these cases, twice the normal period of time as in private industry. I was feeling great about my ventures, but in the back of my mind there remained a vast emptiness. I felt like working at Rikers and Bellevue were part-time jobs, a burden to me that I couldn't get rid of without feeling depressed.

CHAPTER 17

I had a strange feeling that I was going to get busted. Headlines in the *New York Post*, *Daily News*, and *New York Times* would be splashed across their front pages, "Jailhouse therapist busted for selling drugs." I could never live that down. When you are doing these sort of nefarious activities, you cannot write anything down, especially nothing that could incriminate you. So I tried keeping it in my head, but not even a genius could manage such vast amount of financial undertaking and be accurate. I needed to formulate an accounting process. I asked a fellow worker to help me develop and implement a form of bookkeeping.

I approached Michelle Tavarez, a tall skinny white girl married to a Latino, with a business deal. She had just returned from maternity leave, and there was a vulnerability I could exploit. The cost of rearing a baby could run into the hundreds of thousands of dollars. I knew she needed help, and I was willing to give it to her.

It had been over a year since she transferred into our department. She was in her office working on the computer, dressed in a colorful flowery blouse and jeans, nothing fancy. A down-to-earth hippie type of girl who loved music and refused to use makeup. She had her office plastered with pictures of Joe, the father of her brand-new daughter.

"Michelle, would you like to make a couple dollars?" I asked her. It was a bad approach on my part. I didn't explain myself properly. It was kind of shocking to her.

She had heard that I was in business but didn't really know what I was doing. She appeared somewhat nervous when I first made the request for help.

"I don't think I really want to get involved with someone's personal life at the job," she said initially.

"Okay, my bad," I told her as I walked away with my tail between my legs, feeling embarrassed. I didn't mean to startle her with my forwardness. I wasn't accustomed to being turned down on a business deal, especially by women.

Later that afternoon she called my office and left a message on my answering machine. "Could you call me back? This is Michelle," she said.

I didn't return her call. I was afraid she was not the person who could help me out with my present predicament. I was paranoid about everyone around me. I didn't know who could be a potential enemy willing to expose my illegal activities for their personal gain or who my enemy was.

I had to be cautious about people I dealt with. They didn't have my best interest in mind. Michelle was not a person I knew well. She could take me down.

"Rubildo, why didn't you call me back?" she asked as I walked in the hallway getting ready to sign out for the day.

"I thought you made yourself clear, you didn't want to get involved in my business," I said.

"You kind of surprised me, I wasn't prepared to make a decision right then and there. I needed to think about it for a little bit," she said.

"So what are you saying, are you interested?" I said.

"I may be," she said, "but I'm gonna need more details."

I told her, "I'm running a little late right now, so we'll sit down, maybe go to lunch, and discuss it further."

The next morning she came looking for me. I had just gotten off the elevator on the nineteenth floor, where the Bellevue Hospital prison ward is located. She was standing adjacent to my left side by the elevator bank. I knew she was there to see me.

"How are you, Mrs. Tavarez?" I asked.

"Please call me Michelle, we don't have to be formal," she said.

"What time is good for lunch?" I asked.

"That's what I came to tell you. Mrs. Marace gave me a special project and is due by today," she said. "I'm working through my lunch hour, overtime, which I really need."

I told her, "Do whatever you think is best, we can always have lunch on another day."

She appeared somewhat disappointed that I would cancel our lunch date so abruptly. She was not assertive, kind of submissive. Her body language did not demonstrate confidence. But I knew she was trying to open up to me. This went against her rules of work contact. She was very private.

"Can I make a suggestion?" she asked.

"Of course," I said with excitement, hoping that we could work this thing out before the day was done.

"Why don't we order in," she suggested, "and during my lunch hour we could try to work this thing out. What do you think?"

I said, "It sounds like plan to me. Will Chinese be all right with you?"

"Chinese will be fine," she said.

By now everyone in our department knew her lunch hour was at 1:00, so I ordered the food at 12:30. The delivery guy was at Bellevue's lobby at 12:50. You could set your clock by their efficiency. I got to her office at one o'clock on the nose. I always like to be on time.

"Good afternoon, Michelle," I said as I knocked on the door to her office.

"Hi, Mr. Rubildo," she said. "How's your day been so far?"

"Not much to talk about, same routine every day," I told her.

She offered me a folding chair, which she kept behind her office door. There was office and art supplies crowding the place. I barely fit. I placed the Chinese food on top of a nearby desk. She went to one of the cabinets and pulled out paper plates.

"What did you get?" she asked.

"Dumpling and pork fried rice," I told her.

"I'm not really hungry, so you can pack my meal of beef and broccoli and take it home."

"You're going to let me eat by myself?" she asked in an inquisitive tone of voice. "Eat something."

I told her, "I just want to give you my plan so you can review it. We'll get back together tomorrow and you can tell me how you feel about it. I know you're busy, and I don't want to take up any more of your time." I handed her two yellow sheets of paper where I had written down my proposal the night before. A bookkeeping synopsis of what I wanted to create. The next morning we met by the ground floor elevator banks and rode up to the twenty-first floor, where her office was located. While we were by ourselves, in the privacy of her office, she said, "I will work with you and develop a bookkeeping schematic that will keep track of everything you do with your finances."

She had worked in a doctor's office years ago as a bookkeeper, so she had knowledge of this system. I told her, "If anything ever happens to me, you'll have to deny any knowledge of my dealings. Protect yourself."

I never told her what I was into. I didn't want to get her involved in my illegal activities. She was able to make a nice income during this time.

CHAPTER 18

By now I had seventy to eighty clients, not to mention the seven cokehead psychiatrists pretending to be Sigmund Freud buying three and a half grams on a weekly basis, looking for the ultimate high.

An elevator operator who called himself Primo ran a loan shark operation from the basement to the twenty-second floor at Bellevue Hospital. It was genius in scope. Someone would call him and say, "I'm waiting for you on the fifteenth floor."

He would shoot his elevator to the designated floor, collect his money, and run back down to the ground floor without anyone being aware of what was going on. I was impressed with this method of doing business.

"Primo," he told me, "there's enough room for everybody, don't worry about anything, my brother. If I can help you with my elevator, let me know. I'll even collect for you. I always liked you. You present yourself in a dignified way, someone with class."

I was a little concerned about Primo's motives. "Are you sure this will not interfere with your personal business?" I asked.

"Give me a break," he said. "There are over five thousand people working at Bellevue. I can't cover everyone who needs a loan, but the elevator service is going to cost you."

No one will ever give you anything for free. There's always a payoff waiting to be collected somewhere down the line.

I asked Primo, "What is your charge for helping me out?"

Primo was not aware I had multiple business practices going on at Bellevue that would probably overwhelm him. He thought it was just a lending practice. When I told him, "I have different types of businesses going on," he quickly replied, "We have to make new arrangements."

Initially, he gave me the "I like you" routine, but in the long run, he loved money more. That's the beauty of being in business; you make, bend, or break the rules to solve problems. Primo had no qualms helping me out, but to close the deal, he had to get paid.

Primo and I began to work together, utilizing the elevator non-stop. This tall, dark, well-built, handsome Indian-looking South American Ecuadorian was a real hustler.

Once he familiarized himself with my customers, he took complete charge of the collection system. Primo had the elevator running up and down all day long. He loved to be in control; it was like a drug that gave him a special high.

Our relationship lasted several years until cameras became omnipresent throughout the institution. Primo's elevator surfing became obsolete once these intrusive cameras became commonplace.

Bellevue's micromanaging policies by the new administration wouldn't want peddlers to make cash on hospital grounds, their turf, unless they scored a significant profit. This intrusive surveillance made our partnership impossible to continue, so Primo and I parted ways.

CHAPTER 19

Dr. Sloane was a big flamer. He would let everybody know he was a homosexual. He loved to sniff cocaine. He would have gay orgies with all of his buddies, and he needed a lot of powder cocaine. He had an insatiable appetite for this drug. He would lick it like a melting ice cream cone.

The patients didn't respect him. They knew he was gay and would yell in the hallways of Bellevue Hospital prison ward, "Heeeere cooooomes Dr. Homo!" I hadn't told him I was in the business, because he had a big mouth. I was afraid he would expose me. He was always bragging about himself, trying to be the center of attention. This was a forensic psychiatrist with boundary issues. He had no filter. He spent half of this working day criticizing people around him, making fun of them. But this was a highly intelligent individual who had a perfect score on his SATs.

On occasion I would consult with Dr. Vincent Sloane and discuss the intricacies of a criminal mind. But he always had a different agenda.

"Dr. Sloane," I asked, "what do you think about our latest patient who came in on a multiple-murder charge?"

The patient had gone on a bloody rampage, slaughtering both of his parents, three neighbors, and a German shepherd dog. He shot them to death. He then waved down a yellow cab. When he got in, he took out a knife and stabbed the cabbie in the neck. He ran into the subway system, where he jumped headfirst into an oncoming train in a suicide attempt.

Strangely enough, he survived and spent two months convalescing in the medical prison ward at Bellevue. He later was transferred to our prison unit located on the same floor, for a 730 psychiatric evaluation.

Andy Strand was a young white male whose forehead looked horrible. It had taken the brunt of the collision with the train. He required over three hundred stitches to put him back together again. It was a miraculous job performed by the surgeons.

I wasn't sure how to interview this guy. His crime was so unconscionable it left me baffled. Something about these individuals leaves you dispirited, unable to properly decipher the motives behind their actions. I had worked with these individuals for over four decades, and I still struggle to make sense of why someone would want to kill their parents.

Dr. Sloane asked me to bring the patient to the interview room.

As I began walking out of his office, he said, "I want to talk to you after we finish with the patient."

I knew what he wanted to talk with me about. I was going to deny knowing anything about that business. He couldn't be trusted to be in my secret circle of cocaine customers.

This initial interview by Dr. Sloane was not a 730 evaluation. That would come later when two forensic psychiatrists would sit down to determine the patient's competency to stand trial.

Most high-profile cases were handled by Dr. Levine, but he was on vacation during this time, and Dr. Sloane was in charge of our unit. It always seemed that whenever Dr. Sloane was in charge of our service, things would collapse. Nursing didn't like him at all, not because he was gay, but because he was unable to make proper decisions.

Bellevue Hospital's criminally insane unit is a very complicated, unique political entity that requires leadership beyond Dr. Sloane's ability.

He always managed to make the biggest blunders possible while in charge of our forensic unit. Instead of addressing the patient's needs, he was more concerned about whether he could be my customer.

Addicts are always seeking a better deal. Dr. Sloane was no different. After the interview was completed, he asked, "Can you come into my office please."

It took us a few minutes to get past the gates and into the suite where his office was located. "I understand that you are the source of our cocaine connection," he said as he sat down on a light brown leather swivel chair.

"Where did you get that information?" I asked, trying to look surprised.

"Don't play with me," he said. "I'm having a party this weekend, and I need a half ounce of coke."

I was emphatic in my response to him. "I'm sorry to disappoint you, but I don't do that kind of business."

He became incredulous, throwing a pen across the room in frustration. He had a short fuse. He was known to lose his cool easily. I, on the other hand, remained calm, although a little disturbed by his childish reaction. His drug buddies weren't around, and he was in a panic to get a supply of decent coke.

Psychiatrists are an odd group of professionals. They are egotistical, self-centered, drug-seeking caricatures lost in a malaise of inconsistency. What do they produce that's tangible? Everything is esoteric, eclectic, with no solid foundation. They try to mystify an irrational subject matter by making you feel incompetent with fancy phrases such as "What do you mean by that? What are you trying to say?"

Working with the criminally insane never interrupted my judgment. I was alert and in control of all my faculties.

Under constitutional mandates, you're innocent till proven guilty. In other democracies such as France, you are guilty till you are proven innocent. This is a gorgeous concept, to give you the ability to fight your case. I had to get back to the fundamentals, embrace what made me feel comfortable. I had regard for human life.

If I began using my own product, there would be tragic consequences for stepping beyond the imaginary line everyone warned you about. In the movie *Scarface*, Tony Montana was told by Frank, "Never use your own supply." The first thing you lose when you start to drug and drink is your spirituality. You develop an "I don't give a fuck" attitude. I don't give a fuck if I have to use the F train as my mattress, pillow, and blanket at two o'clock in the morning. I don't care if I see people coming in and they feel they are in the presence of a derelict. I don't give a fuck if I lose my job tomorrow. I don't give a fuck if I don't see my family for long periods of time. I don't give a fuck if I get arrested tonight. I don't give a fuck if I lose my mind. The only thing I gave a fuck about is my next high. Fortunately, I caught myself before it got beyond my control.

CHAPTER 20

I often remember Jimmy, who lived a few doors from my house. He was a top-notch mechanic who worked with luxury cars. On the East Coast of the United States there were four garages who specialized in expensive automobiles such as top-of-the-line Benz, Jags, BMWs, and supercars.

Jimmy, who had migrated from Costa Rica with chump change in his pocket, was living the American dream. He was always dressed in greasy overalls with a tool in his hand at all times, ready to fix any mechanical instrument. He stood about six feet three inches tall with immense arms and shoulders and an eighteen-inch neck. He could have played American football, and middle linebacker would had been a natural position for him. He owned a house, had three children, a great woman, and two cars, and made $2,000 per week, plus tips. If I owned a Mercedes-Benz and you were working on it, I would throw you $100 as a tip, not a problem.

One Sunday night, Jimmy knocked on my door and asked to borrow $50. He looked disheveled, bleary eyed. He had a three-day beard growth, and he smelled like three hundred camel farts. I was flabbergasted. Here was a guy that was making nice money asking me for a loan. I didn't question his request. I gave him the cash. I couldn't get Jimmy out of my mind that night. He looked and smelled terrible. I could tell Jimmy had been on a three-day run. The next day he stopped by around seven thirty Monday evening and tried to give me $75. I told him, "Just give me my fifty bucks." He had cleaned up and was looking like himself again. The week went by quickly, and I was preparing my clothes for work that Sunday evening when Jimmy came back seeking for another loan, this time $100. Jimmy was bringing home close to $4,000 a week, an unconscionable amount for an individual who couldn't read or write.

I asked him, "What's wrong Jimmy?"

Jimmy knew I was a therapist. There was a confidentiality privilege that cannot be severed or bridged. Jimmy told me, "I met a girl that loved to fuck me in a special way." She was a crackhead who turned him on. All his money between Friday and Sunday went to servicing her addiction. Jimmy lost everything, his house, his wife, his children, his cars, his mind. I saw Jimmy on Roosevelt Avenue eating out of garbage cans, and I couldn't say hello because I knew he would ask me for $10.

CHAPTER 21

The most gruesome case I was ever involved with was Anthony Martin. This guy had a lot of personal issues. His mother, an ugly, stinky, drug-addicted whore desperate for cash who would suck anybody's dick for $5. She was asked by a drug cartel doing business in the tristate area to deliver a kilo of cocaine to a specific place somewhere in New York City. She had bundled up her five-year-old child in an umbrella stroller as part of her disguise. She thought wrapping up an innocent child in blankets would make her immune to transport hard narcotics. Unfortunately, SWAT raided the place at the same time, and she got busted. Under the Rockefeller laws, she was facing at least fifteen years in prison. Often individuals are turned down on their first parole hearing, so she would have to do at least seventeen years. She handed the five-year-old child over to her mother to raise. This was back in 1969.

By the time he was seventeen years old, crack cocaine hit New York City like an atom bomb. Communities were under siege, destroyed by this epidemic. Breaking and entering became the norm.

Life was cheap, over two thousand murders were committed per year during this five year time frame. The jail system swelled to over fifteen thousand inmates. An unimaginable amount of people were swallowed up and victimized by this new smokable form of cocaine. There was not enough room to house this growing population at

Rikers Island, so they used the gym. A makeshift dorm was set up by the corrections department to accommodate this increase in inmates. If within twenty-four hours at Rikers you didn't have a bed, it would cost the city $120 a day. Part of their solution was bus therapy. Ride these motherfuckers around till a bed was made available to avoid this payout.

Anthony Martin killed his grandmother, who raised him from childhood, stabbed her seventeen times and had sex with the body for over a three-day period. When the corpse got too stiff and he was not enjoying himself, he got angry. He punched the lifeless body repeatedly in frustration and threw it out the window like it was a piece of trash. Later, he would sign himself into Kirby, a state hospital. After a two-month stay at this facility, detectives were waiting outside and arrested him for murder in the second degree. He'd been bouncing from Rikers to Bellevue to Kirby for over thirty years without a resolution to his case. He claimed the insanity defense. A week before he was to start trial, he would stop taking his medication and decompensate into a psychotic state. Martin was a terror when he was nineteen years old, intimidating all the clinical staff. Regardless of how menacing he was, I nevertheless asked him, "Do you want to talk?"

He told me, "I don't talk to the devil. You need to stay the fuck away from me. I hate white people."

I said, "I'm Puerto Rican, born on the island an original native."

"You may have been born there, but you're still a white devil trying to oppress the black man," he said in an angry tone.

"While you're here at Bellevue, you have to treat me with respect and be a gentleman, it doesn't cost anything," I told him in an authoritative voice.

His response was totally negative and evil in nature. "You will get my respect when you let me fuck your mother in the ass and you suck my cock, my twelve-inch cock."

I shot back with a snide remark. "You gonna owe her six inches, motherfucker, because you are half the man I thought you were."

He was incredulous because I didn't feel intimidated by his stupid bullshit. "You keep fucking with me and I'm going to break your shit up, you better step away and do yourself a favor," he said while trying to stare me down. His spit splattering on my face. By now other patients were gathering around us in the recreational room, waiting to see if there would be a fight. I was vulnerable. Officer Perez had left the area, leaving me alone with this pack of wolves. I had just started working at the prison ward, and my skills were weak. I had no idea how to handle this situation, but I knew I couldn't show fear.

"Listen, Martin, I didn't bring you here. I'm just trying to help you, but if you don't want my help, the heck with you. Give me a fucking break," I finally told him. I turned to the gathering crowd of inmates hoping to see a fight fest and said, "All right, the shows over, let's break this shit up."

It would take over seven years to finally break into Martin's personal space. Over the years Martin began to lose his edge. He was no longer the defiant, egotistical, self-centered Five Percenter (a quasi-Islamic sect) that he claimed to be. I first met him back in 1985. He went out of his way to talk to me now. "Mr. Rubildo, how you been doing?" he said, looking to see if I would be receptive to his approach.

"How are you doing, Martin?" I asked him. I've known Martin over thirty years. He's been locked up at Kirby Hospital. He won't be coming out for the rest of his life.

CHAPTER 22

John Wright, known as the Beast, wanted to be in the crack cocaine business. He and a few of his buddies decided to confiscate the apartment of an elderly woman who lived alone. During a home invasion, he bludgeoned her to death and threw her body in the East River. He then quickly set up shop and began slinging dime bags from her apartment. His plan was running so well he began to look for second place to expand his business. The next victim was an elderly man who lived in the same Upper West Side project.

By now the elderly woman's body had been found floating in the East River. Since it was ruled a homicide by the medical examiner's office, detectives began an investigation. Clues were left behind that enabled detectives to track down where she lived. Police were able to find out that her apartment was being used as a drug den. Strange people coming in and out at all hours of the night. They set up surveillance and raided the place. They busted five people with half a kilo of cocaine and two Uzi machine guns.

One of the detainees spilled the beans on the Beast, who was busy dismembering the body of the elderly man. He laid the corpse in the bathtub, where he was trying to cut him apart with an ineffective butcher knife. The most difficult part was the head decapitation, where he struggled for hours to separate the head from the body. He then wandered around the apartment with the head underneath his arm, holding it like it was a football. He was in a psychotic, delusional state when the police knocked on the door. He looked through the peephole and knew he was about to be arrested for murder. When he didn't answer, the police had no choice but to knock down the door. After entering the premises, he asked the police if they were looking for him or this guy, pointing to the head. He was handcuffed, charged, read his rights, and dragged off to Bellevue Hospital for a psych evaluation. That was standard procedure for any individual who committed a horrific crime in the five boroughs of New York City.

I went up to Mr. Wright and introduced myself. "How are you doing, sir? My name is Mr. Rubildo." I informed him that I was the therapist on the unit.

"You could call me the Beast, that's my nickname," he said with an air of arrogance that immediately rubbed me the wrong way. Here was a guy who murdered two people in cold blood and showed no remorse. "No, Mr. Wright," I told him, "it would be inappropriate for me to use your nickname when I'm addressing you."

He was a 250-pound-obese, imposing figure who had no soul. As soon as he arrived at Bellevue Hospital for a psych evaluation, he became the talk of the unit. We had another high-profile patient on our hands, and the news media vans, two dozen of them, were lining up on First Avenue. They were on a mission to gather as much information as possible from our staff. There was always someone willing to betray the trust of our unit.

Dr. Levine was back in high alert, telling the staff to be careful about providing any kind of information that would be detrimental to our unit.

My judgment was always a little clouded whenever I spoke to Mr. Wright, the Beast, as he would like to call himself.

"Mr. Wright, are you aware of your charges?" I asked him.

"I didn't do this bullshit," he claimed. "They are trying to pin a murder or two on me," he said.

I was hoping to get more information about his background. He was very talkative in the beginning. "Did you do these murders?" I asked him.

"I was trying to start a business," he said. "I don't know what they're talking about."

"What sort of upbringing did you have?" I asked him.

"Why is that important?" he said.

"When your lawyer goes to defend you, these are the things that he would want to know. It's all part of the strategy he'll be presenting on your behalf," I explained to him.

When you're arrested and charged with murder, it doesn't immediately sink in. It's difficult to wrap your brain around the fact that you'll be going away for a long period of time. After a few weeks of chemical and verbal intervention, Mr. Wright was beginning to feel a lot better. He was running around the unit interacting well with his peers.

When I walked into the unit, he ran right up to me and said, "I have a good idea." He was excited, animated. I couldn't wait to hear what he had to say. "What's your great idea?" I asked. While on our forensic unit, the Beast wanted to know if he could sell his story so he could put money in a commissary account. I almost fell off my chair when he made that suggestion. This guy had no clue. Clearly he had numerous psychiatric issues that needed to be addressed with chemical intervention. I tried to explain to him that according to the Son of Sam laws, you cannot profit from you criminal activities. He was unable to comprehend this concept. He was constantly on the phone, calling publishing houses, trying to sell his story. Unfortunately for him, no one was interested due to the mandates of the Son of Sam laws.

It took a few months to stabilize this patient, and we sent him to Rikers Island, where I ran into him. He pranced over to me and attempted to give me a hug. "This is not a social reunion," I told him. "I'm just glad to see you, Mr. Rubildo. I didn't know you worked here too," he said. He was housed in mod 11 B, the most dangerous place in New York City. He had joined the vicious, callous Bloods gang and fitted right in. They would terrorize anybody they didn't like, mostly helpless individuals who couldn't defend themselves.

He was still trying to peddle his story to anyone who would listen. He was found fit to stand trial and eventually was convicted of a double homicide, drug trafficking, and other lesser charges. He is now serving a lifetime sentence without the possibility of parole.

CHAPTER 23

Court proceedings are difficult for your average layperson to understand.

The legal field is esoteric in nature with many convoluted entities that can confuse even seasoned attorneys. The interpretation of the law is constantly changing and evolving. One minute you are charged with second-degree murder; the next moment it's negligent homicide.

These individuals at Rikers who played the insanity defense card are basically trying to get their charges reduced. In an era that has gone by a long time ago, this was a common practice. Today it's almost impossible to utilize the insanity defense; it just doesn't work anymore. In rare, extreme cases, this type of defense has some validity, but for the most part it is useless. Corrupt psychiatrists and lawyers were the reason for its demise.

Defense attorneys would pay doctors $10,000 to $15,000 as professional witness to ensure that their client was found unfit to stand trial. Today you need two doctors to agree on the patient's mental status in order to proceed.

Money always has a tendency to alter people's thinking. Doctors are no different. If I'm offered a stipend of $10,000 to $15,000, it may cloud my judgment.

There are always exceptions to the rule. I'm not going to place every doctor and lawyer under the same umbrella of corruption. There is a large number of doctors and lawyers who practice their profession with integrity and would never sell out for a few gold pieces.

But wave a few dollars in front of anybody and the corrupt human nature ingrained into our DNA will quickly manifest itself. Go to any amusement park in the United States and you probably have to wait two hours for a ride. Pay a nominal $25 fee and you'll be allowed to go in front of the line. This is a corruption by the amusement industry to get into your pocket. Children have a low tolerance. They need to be gratified immediately, and this amusement industrial complex knows how to capitalize on parents' inadequacies.

I've been in contact with doctors and lawyers all of my professional career, and I've yet to find one of them that would not bite on a financial gift. Even at Bellevue Hospital, I've yet to find someone who's not willing to take a bribe.

CHAPTER 24

I had to diversify into legal businesses in order to launder the money. I couldn't put it in the bank. It would bring too much attention to my account, and the feds were always lurking, looking for someone to make a mistake and they'd confiscate your cash. Once they put their hands on it, you'll never get it back.

But before I ventured into turning this ill-gotten booty into legit establishments, I had to create a personal uniform that would identify me as a seasoned clinician. I decided to become the best-dressed gentlemen at Bellevue and Rikers Island. I bought eighty suits, a thousand ties, two hundred shirts, eighty suspenders, five hundred pairs of shoes, sixty hats, and enough cologne to choke an elephant.

Robert De Niro came to my job to research a part for a movie called *Analyze This*. He had been there a few years before to research the movie *Backdraft* also. Dr. Benjamin Levine had a lot of connections in the movie industry. Richard Gere and then Peter Berg made a thirteen-episode TV series about our doctors, and I was used as an extra and a technical adviser.

Robert De Niro was an unassuming guy. He wore a wrinkled shirt, black jeans, and sneakers, and his hair was uncombed. This was not the type of image I was accustomed to seeing of this powerful actor. When he arrived on our forensic unit, he was surrounded by the correction officers for protection purposes. There was an additional group of twenty-three administrators following him around vying for a position to get his autograph. Our forensic unit had turned into a big circus.

"Good afternoon, Mr. De Niro," I said. "Welcome to our friendly abode."

"Happy to be here," he said.

I told him, "Let's walk back to the dayroom, that's where we are going to have the discussion group."

I had one of the nurses announce on the overhead page that the group was about to start. I knew that because of the large crowd gathering in the dayroom, we would have logistic problems. The whole hospital was abuzz when word spread that Robert De Niro would be on the forensic unit.

This was highly unusual to have celebrities in a patient area. Dr. Levine had made all the arrangements to make this happen. He had juice.

Between administrators, support staff, and patients, we had nearly eighty people in the back of the dayroom, where all of our activities took place. It was so crowded that we had to recruit chairs from other units to accommodate everybody; it was a zoo.

One of our patients, once we made a circle with the chairs, yelled out to Mr. De Niro, "Could you bail me out?"

Everyone burst out in laughter except me. I was beginning to lose control of this crowd.

"Don Corleone," another patient, shouted out, "Make me an offer that I can't refuse."

Things were beginning to get out of hand. I needed to get control again. I decided to place a small circle of patients inside this large bubble of insignificant administrators.

After the group was completed, Mr. De Niro was escorted off the unit and into our conference room. We spent the next fifteen minutes reviewing the content of the discussion group.

"I apologize for the distraction caused by our personnel," I told him.

"It's understandable," he said. "You have a very interesting job. If you ever complete any kind of literary work concerning this population, give me a call. I'll look it over."

"I would appreciate that, thank you very much," I told him.

We then walked to the elevator banks and said our good-byes, and he disappeared.

In the movie *Don't Say a Word*, I was picked up in front of my house by a chauffeur-driven stretch limousine and taken to LaGuardia Airport, where an electronic first-class ticket was waiting for me. I was then flown to Toronto, where I was a technical adviser for a Michael Douglas movie. Another limo was waiting for me when I got there. The driver was holding up a sign with my name, RUBILDO. I was put up in a five-star hotel. The bed was as big as a football field and the bath tub a mini swimming pool. I was living large.

It's unbelievable that I was paid $3,000 for telling people what to do and an additional $300 for meals and extras. But that's the movie industry. Everything is first class. Unfortunately, the movie came out a week after the terrorist attack on the Twin Towers, and not many people felt like going to the movies at that time.

When Robert De Niro came to Bellevue to sit in on my discussion group, I was sitting on top of the world. I never thought such good fortune would be bestowed on me. The best actor on the planet calling on me for advice.

CHAPTER 25

I had drawers full of cash. I had to invest in things other than illegal enterprises. I went down to Puerto Rico and bought two properties in a matter of a few days. I was now a landlord. I knew from my paralegal days that property never goes down in value. Back in New York I opened a dry-cleaning store with brand-new equipment, hired a girl to run it, and soon began to make money.

Patricia, who ran the dry-cleaning store on Eighty-Second Street, between First and Second Avenue, was a hardworking, beautiful girl who had migrated from Honduras fifteen years ago. She was a seamstress by trade and a stickler for details.

This kind of business calls for itemizing hundreds of garments per month. She was required to keep close track of everything that came in and out of the store.

Soon after my alarm would go off at five o'clock in the morning, I would call her. This was a signal for her to start getting ready. I would pick her up by 6:15 a.m. in front of the building where she lived.

I wanted to make a deal with Patricia in order for me to become anonymous. I wanted to become a silent partner. This way, nothing could be traced back to me. When people come from the other side of the world, they are willing to take a risk or chance. She agreed. I signed the store over to her, and placed it under her name. I told her, "I will sell you the store for a dollar, but I would have to gain certain

83

privileges." Patricia looked confused, and she tried to make sense out of what I was saying. "What do you mean Don Marcel?" she asked.

"First," I told her, "I would get my clothes dry-cleaned for free. Second, you would have to let me clean some illegal money through the store."

She looked puzzled. I knew she didn't understand the washing or laundering of the money. She was not a street-savvy person. In fact, she was a very religious girl who went to church with her family every Sunday.

"What do you mean by washing illegal money?" she asked.

"You have to keep this conversation strictly between us," I told her. "You cannot mention this to anybody."

She asked, "Can I get in trouble?"

"Yes, you can," I told her. "Technically, you could lose everything."

"So why would I take such a chance?" she asked. "I have a new-born who depends on me."

"I'm going to give you a very good deal," I told her. "I will subsidize your rent for the next six months. In addition, I will give you a 10 percent commission on all the cash being cleansed by the store. Afterward, I will increase your commission to 15 percent for washing the money."

I knew she was still perplexed about my proposal to jeopardize her freedom. It didn't sit well with her.

She continued to badger me about this proposal, whether she could go to jail. I told her, "If you can't handle this situation, let me know. I'll get somebody else."

We formed an alliance of convenience. She never questioned my veracity to make money for her family.

Whenever Patricia got into my car in the early morning at 6:15 a.m., she would say, "Thank you, Don Marcel," a form of respect for letting her make a living that would help her family. Women would sell their ass to help their children succeed.

CHAPTER 26

Shortly after getting back from Puerto Rico, the *New York Post* had a sensational headline. A man had killed his ballerina girlfriend, chopped her into little pieces, cooked her into a stew, and fed it to the homeless in the Lower East Side of Manhattan. If you commit such a horrific crime, you'll be sent to Bellevue for a psychiatric evaluation. Sure enough, David G. was placed on 19 W to see if he was competent to stand trial. Dr. Levine and Dr. Barkley would make the determination. In the meantime, our job was to make sure none of their rights were violated. Under the New York State Criminal Procedure Law (CPL) Article 730 an evaluation is conducted by two psychiatrists to determine whether an individual lacks the capacity to understand the proceedings against him or if he can assist in his own defense. Does he know the role of a judge? Can he assist a lawyer to defend his actions? Can he be innocent due to reason of insanity?

When Mr. G arrived at Bellevue Hospital for a 730 competency evaluation to determine his ability to stand trial, he was disheveled, catatonic, and nonverbal. He was in acute distress.

Dr. Levine, the unit chief and director of the forensic service, ordered that he be heavily sedated for the next forty-eight hours. This was standard procedure for individuals who committed horrific crimes. Most individuals charged with this type of gruesome murders remain in a fog for a couple of days, weeks, and in some rare cases, years. They're in shock. It takes time for things to sink in. That they may be going away for a long time becomes their main concern.

I had to approach Mr. G with caution according to Dr. Levine.

I went into Dr. Benjamin Levine's office and asked him, "So what are we supposed to do with this guy?"

He said, "We have to treat him like any other patient on our list, but be aware that there'll be a lot of questions asked about him. The *New York Post* is waiting outside my office right now to discuss this guy."

The staff was always being told and prepped not to say anything about our patients. Dr. Levine said, "There will be reporters hanging around trying to use you, be careful."

After Mr. G came out of his chemically induced coma, he began to verbalize his feelings concerning his recent actions. Most individuals are initially stunned when they realize they are being charged with murder. The mind has difficulty grasping this notion.

"Mr. G," I asked him, "how are you feeling?"

He was still mildly sedated. "I'm feeling all right," he said while drooling from the right side of his mouth.

I asked him, "Are you aware of your charges?"

He was somewhat confused and unable to respond immediately. After a few moments, he said, "What charges?"

I waited for a few seconds before I told him, "You've been charged with second-degree murder of Valerie Wright. Do you know her?"

He was still under the stupor of sedation, but it appeared he recognized the name. "Val," he said, "is my girlfriend."

I said to him, "When was the last time you saw her?"

He was still in a daze from all the medication Dr. Levine had administered in his initial treatment. "I'm not sure the last time I saw her," he stated while slurring his speech.

He was sitting in a green plastic chair nodding out when I told him, "We'll talk later when you're in better control of your mental faculties." He jerked his head back, opened his eyes, and asked, "What did you say!" I repeated what I just told him. "We'll talk later when you're in better control of your mental faculties."

He appeared befuddled and asked, "Who are you anyway?"

I told him, "My name is Mr. Rubildo. I'm a therapist at Bellevue prison ward. You're here for a psych evaluation on a second-degree murder charge. Dr. Levine will be treating you."

He was incoherent and unable to understand the magnitude of his charges. As I got up from my chair, I told him, "I'll talk to you later." He went back to nodding out and didn't respond to my statement.

I walked into the nurses' station and told the nurse in charge, "Perhaps it's better that we place this man in his room, he may fall and crack his head open." As I made my way past the front gates, I saw two orderlies escorting Mr. G back to his room.

When I went into Dr. Levine's office, he was in panic control mode. He said, "There are over ten media vans parked in front of the hospital." He warned everybody on his staff, "You are not to talk to any reporters concerning this case. You will be fired on the spot."

This was a murder that placed the whole city on high alert. What kind of individual would kill and then cook a human being? People who knew me would come up and ask, "Do you have that guy who cooked the ballerina girlfriend and handed it out to the Lower East Side of Manhattan homeless population as a stew?" I would tell them in the most cordial way possible, "I can't talk about that to anyone." Investigative reporters had flooded Bellevue Hospital. They were everywhere, making inquiries about the status of this individual. Some of them knew me from prior similar cases and bum-rushed me one afternoon after leaving work.

"Mr. Rubildo, Mr. Rubildo, can you tell us something about Mr. G?" they shouted.

"I'm sorry, ladies and gentlemen of the press, but we are under strict orders not to discuss this particular case or any other case with the press," I explained to them. But there's always one or two individuals who would leak out information concerning our patients for a small reward. Sure enough, the next day New York City tabloids were ablaze with all sorts of information concerning Mr. G. Things that only our staff would be privy to. Dr. Levine was so angry he was throwing things across the office. He had a staff meeting and yelled, "Don't let me find out who did this, I will have their heads." It took a couple of days until he finally calmed down.

I sat with Mr. G a few more times to discuss his case before he was finally transferred to a state hospital.

CHAPTER 27

In 1963, my best friend Carl Santiago was killed, murdered by a drunk driver. His neck snapped, killing him instantly. He didn't suffer. He was thrown 160 feet from the impact. I was devastated. The funeral left me with a void I'm unable to fill to this day. This motherfucker was given two tickets, for speeding and driving under the influence. Carl Santiago was my friend, and the driver was only given two tickets. What kind of justice was that?

Santiago's lifelong dream was to be a professional football player. He was a talented, gifted punter who worked endless hours at his craft. He always carried a pigskin and pretended to kick it away into the end zone of the Giants stadium in the Bronx. That was his fantasy, a dream he wanted to accomplish before he died.

We would hang out for hours talking about our future while listening to the Platters, the coolest, most outstanding R&B group at that time.

"Rubildo, when I hit the big times, I'm taking you with me," he would always tell me.

"Don't worry, I'll be your agent," I would quickly reply. "I'll protect your interest."

Santiago and I, we became blood brothers, and I still have the scar on my wrist, a fading reminder of our friendship. To this day I can't watch a football game without recalling this fantastic guy.

In the law, it is all about intent. What was going through the person's mind during the commission of the offense? If you walk into a bodega with a gun and while you are robbing the place you shoot and kill the clerk, that is murder in the second degree. In a similar scenario, if you rob the place without a weapon and the clerk dies in a struggle with you, it would be a lesser charge. Since your intent was different at the time. Both are murders, but the intent in the second scenario doesn't rise to the necessary level to justify a second-degree murder. Mens rea is a description of the mental state of an individual during the commission of a crime. Usually violent encounters such as murder, arson, rape, and pedophilia are felonies that carry large amounts of prison time. Psychiatrists who are most of the time under the influence of powdered cocaine are given the unique task to determine whether these individuals can proceed. Psychiatry is an inexact science with numerous flaws that has very little commonality in reality. You cannot measure it. The results are unpredictable, and we have to depend on the judgment of fools.

Would I go to a psychiatrist and spill my guts about my personal and emotional issues? I would have to be crazy. They don't serve any purpose other than lining their pockets, and I can understand that. Money is always a great motivator. I could appreciate their gimmick since I was doing the same thing, making money out of nothing.

CHAPTER 28

I have to give props to Angie. She always had a pint of some type of drink in her desk drawer. She loved her booze. She worked in medical records, a very sensitive place for the personal injury business. If you could get a chart out of Bellevue and copy it, we had a big advantage. Was there a preexisting condition that would nullify a big payoff in a case? This is why people take chances for the big payoff. I gave Angie $100 for her help; my profit was $400. Who the fuck was Angie? Just another cog in a big wheel of my money-making ventures. Angie was just an alcoholic in a long string of fools I used to get what I wanted.

I would take charts out of Bellevue and review them for my purpose, to determine if they were useful to our company. Angie was my kind of girl. She was always blitzed on alcohol and ready to give you a hug at any time. She carried a big bottle of Binaca, the mouthwash, so her breath wouldn't smell of alcohol. But there was no body mint for the poisonous odor coming out of her body. She was a diabetic who was 120 pounds overweight, had elephantiasis of her feet, and refused to take medication in order to drink her Scotch whiskey. She chain-smoked marijuana cigarettes but always had a smile on her face.

"Hey, Rubildo," she would say to me, "you want to have a little drink with me?" She would open her desk drawer in order to show me the bottle of whiskey.

"Now, Angie, you know I work in a very sensitive area, 19 W prison ward. If I get busted, I lose my job," I would tell her.

"You have to learn to live a little," she fired back.

"I tell you what, one day I'll take you out to dinner and we'll have a few drinks together," I told her.

"Promises, promises, promises, you're always telling me that," she said.

"I know, but right now I want to take care of business. You have Jones's and Smith's charts?"

She went to the back area of the department, where she disappeared for a few minutes and returned with a large bag. Inside were the two charts. She then asked me in an apologetic tone of voice, "Can you give me an advance on the money? My liquor is running out." I knew she would ask for an advance. She always needed money.

"Not a problem," I said. I always paid her in full. There was no sense to make her wait for a couple of dollars. I reached into my pocket, pulled out two $100 bills, and handed them over to her.

I needed to rush these charts to the downtown office ASAP. A full set of copies were to be made within an hour and sent back to Bellevue. I called Cancilleri and made him aware that the charts would be sent by bike messenger. "Doctor," I said, "we need these charts back at Bellevue Hospital within the next hour and a half." I had met up with the courier on Twenty-Six Street and First Avenue. When I handed over the packet, I always felt nervous over the years. Angie, with her laid-back attitude, did reassure me that I could take my time. She was always mellow, without a care in the world.

CHAPTER 29

But I was still trying to understand my purpose. Why was I here in the forensic unit at Bellevue Hospital, a great institution in the forefront of psychiatric medicine?

Working with such horrific cases makes you lose your spirituality. It leaves you void of compassion; it makes you callous and indifferent. After a while your mind begins to settle into a new reality. You condition yourself and accept the fact that evil exists and you are in direct contact in its presence. Why would a grown man rape twenty-three children ages five to eight and have no remorse about his actions? We excuse these evil deeds by saying this individual has a mental disease.

What I have to question is, where is the punishment for these actions? In my opinion, castration would be the only suitable remedy for these men. But all of these liberal thinkers, who are never in contact with this type of behavioral dynamics, would come to his rescue, claiming he was mentally incapacitated at the time and he can't be held responsible. Where is the justice for the children who are now scarred for life? He was found not guilty due to diminished capacity and sent to a state hospital to do a few years. For all we know, this guy could be living next door to you. Don't let your small, innocent children play outside unsupervised.

When you look at this dark world, remember that I worked at both Bellevue prison ward and Rikers Island mental observation units, places where even the most seasoned clinician would be shocked by the intense amount of violence. On a daily basis people are injured. I've witnessed fifteen to twenty guys jump one inmate and leaving him in a coma, barely alive. This is not an isolated incident but part of the daily behavior that takes place on the Rock. No one who has been arrested as a sexual predator wants that information to be disclosed. Specially while living in this population. These inmates loath pedophiles; they have an odd morality. Like I said before, everyone gets paid in full right here. You don't have to wait for judgment day to account for your sins.

One day while I was watching the news, a reporter was commenting on this subject matter when without notice this inmate's picture was flashed across the television screen. At the time nearly twenty inmates were in the room. They beat him senselessly. A small amount of justice for these children was served that day. But a few broken teeth, punctured eye, bloody nose, and a cracked skull are barely enough punishment to satisfy the social consciousness. I'm sure that down the road some staff member will out him again and a similar beating will be inflicted on his ass. If he was pretending to be crazy, the fear of potentially getting this type of justice will drive him nuts.

I'm sure that somewhere down the line I'll have to pay in full for my actions. But for now let the band play on.

CHAPTER 30

When Joseph Kennedy made his millions peddling whiskey, the authorities turned a blind eye. He was later rewarded for making the SEC regulations by making $1 for every bottle of whiskey sold in this country. At the time he was the biggest insider trader. That's why he was given the job. He knew how to close the loopholes. People who run the government are the biggest crooks.

He is the guy who manipulated the whole system to get one of his sons elected president.

When it comes to Joseph Kennedy, he's no different from the drug kingpins that run Mexican or Colombian drug cartels. Or for that matter, the Harlem drug dealers or Lower East Side drug runners. It's all based on supply and demand. Joseph Kennedy took advantage of this financial concept.

If there was a financial reward attached to sniffing ass, you'll be surprised how many people would volunteer their services. I admired Kennedy's vision, his fortitude. He was able to see the big picture and pursued it to the end. He was able to get one of his sons elected president of United States, the most powerful person in the world, with dirty money. They came to be known as Camelot, and he was revered for his accomplishments. To this date the Kennedy name is glorified and held in high esteem. He had a great formula for achieving financial independence: give the people what they want, alcohol.

This simple strategy is still in place with different players calling the shots.

Street-level drug dealers will never get rich. They are the victims housed in Rikers Island. They come into the system by the dozen on a daily basis with dreams of making it big in the drug trade.

As long as there are human beings on the planet, there will be a demand for drugs and alcohol. We are all pleasure seekers that can be comforted by these insidious elements.

But in the background, puppeteers are making billions of dollars at the expense of our young generations.

Lieutenant Oliver North allegedly started a crack cocaine epidemic in East LA to fund a war in Central America against the Contras in Nicaragua when the United States refused to allocate any further funding. How about John DeLorean, who was caught on tape trying to sell twenty kilos of cocaine to keep his car company running? How much time did they receive? None.

During John DeLorean's cocaine possession criminal trial back in 1984, it was intimated by his lawyers that he was set up, entrapped with the help of FBI agents in cahoots with governmental entities. He was videotaped in a hotel room picking up a kilo of cocaine and claiming, "This is better than gold." Clearly a reference to how much money could be made with this product. He was planning on selling 100 kilos of cocaine, that's 220 pounds, in a last-ditch effort to save his failing automobile company.

I've known numerous individuals locked up for eight months in Rikers Island for merely having a bag of dope on their person. These individuals don't have expensive, high-powered lawyers to manipulate court proceedings.

Charles Smith, a tall muscular African American was busted with a little over a half ounce of cocaine while walking in the Upper West Side of Manhattan. He was a victim of stop-and-frisk policy of the old Bloomberg administration. The judge gave him a $200,000 bail. Unable to come up with that kind of money, he spent the next three years on Rikers Island fighting his case. In addition, the city had to pony up $75,000 to house this individual on Rikers Island for those three years. His charges were possession with intent to sell. *Criminal enterprise* were the words used by the police to describe his actions.

At the time of his arrest, he was facing fifteen years.

Mr. Smith was a gentle giant, well mannered. You could see that he had good fundamentals provided to him while growing up. He came up to me and asked me if we could talk. It seemed he wanted to get some things off his chest. He had just arrived at one of our mental units from the general population. Apparently he tried to hurt himself.

We sat in a small office located inside the unit. "What's on your mind?" I asked.

"Do you have any idea why I am here?" he asked.

"From what I understand, you're here on a drug charge," I told him.

"That's right, I'm here for drug possession with intent to sell. They're offering me fifteen years," he said.

"I'm not here for your criminal case, I'm here for your mental anguish. Why would you try to hurt yourself?" I told him.

"I didn't try to hurt myself, I just told the doctor I was feeling a little depressed. Wouldn't you be a little depressed if you were locked up in here facing fifteen years?" he said.

"You have to be careful what you tell doctors, they're always trying to protect their license," I told him.

"Anyway," he said, "can you help me get back to the general population?"

"It's not that easy," I told him. "Once you come to a place like this, we have to observe you for few a weeks before we can make a determination on your mental status."

"But I'm not crazy," he stated in a raised voice. He was beginning to get annoyed. Therapists don't always tell you what you want to hear.

"First of all, lower your voice. I'm standing right here in front of you, there's no reason for you to be shouting," I told him.

"My apologies," he said, "but I'm stuck in a place I don't belong."

"I know it could be very frustrating to be in a place like this, but you have to be patient," I told him.

He calmed down, but I knew he wasn't happy with my response. There are hundreds of guys locked up on the Rock in similar circumstances, low-level drug dealers, substance abusers. Individuals who should be in treatment rather than incarcerated.

There are so many inadequacies in the criminal justice system. It is frightening to know anyone could be victimized in this way. John DeLorean busted in a room full of cocaine was able to dance out of court without a scratch. The time has come to think about the unconscionable, the legalization of all drugs.

Why is our government so hell-bent on maintaining heroin, cocaine, marijuana, etc., illegal? Is there an underlying conspiratorial factor in maintaining the status quo? Is the jail and prison system a way of eliminating competition for jobs and resources?

It is estimated that there are to 2.2 million people locked up across the country, with an additional 4.3 million more in police contact, parole, probation, house arrest, etc. 70 percent of these individuals have a substance-abuse pathology. This in itself would be a great incentive for the politicians not to legalize drugs. It would send a shockwave throughout the criminal justice system if drugs were to be legalized. The courts, jails, and prisons would be emptied, and of course it would put lawyers out of business.

Then there is the "eliminating the competition" factor. As a young African American or Latino male is slapped with a felony drug possession charge, he is done. He will lose the privilege of voting and holding a government job and, for that matter, any job. He would be locked out of pursuing the American dream. It's part of the invisible, institutionalized racism embedded in our system. If these governmental laissez-faire type of policies continue to flourish, untold numbers of young generations will be herded into this corrupt system.

There are seventy prisons in New York State with a population of over 77,000 inmates; 12,770 are housed in New York City county jails. As of 2015 New York State has allocated $4.2 billion to house these inmates per year, with hidden costs. The New York City operating budget to house inmates is a little over $3 billion as of 2015. The amount of people who depend on this bloated bureaucracy is staggering. Why would politicians dismantle this lucrative cash cow? Toothpaste, toothbrushes, soap, even the farmer who grows the food are impacted by this system.

Whenever I walk into this area, I feel uncomfortable because I know these guys are pissed. Inmates know they are being abused by a corrupt system that will be in place for many generations.

Did the politicians ever stop to think about the ramifications caused by the introduction of crack cocaine into these communities? The colonel was fighting a guerilla warfare in the jungles of Nicaragua financed by the crack epidemic he was alleged to have started in East L.A.

East LA was a black community with a large influx of Mexican immigrants considered expendable collateral damage, more fodder for the criminal justice system to swallow and throw out like morning garbage.

I'm certain that this plan was not fabricated by Colonel Oliver North alone. He must have been given instructions to carry out this agenda from the highest level of government cronies.

The community remains in turmoil to this day. It will take additional decades to solve the problems apparently caused by Colonel Oliver North.

The propaganda machine tells us that Mr. Kennedy, Mr. DeLorean, and Mr. North are all great Americans. It mattered little that they left whole communities destroyed along the way.

Charles Smith eventually took a plea deal of three and a half to seven years, and I helped him get back to the general population, where he belonged.

But let a Latino or black adolescent get picked up with half a gram of coke and he'll face years behind bars. The government is in everybody's pocket, and they tax the shit out of you and throw the money around like it is garbage. Try to make a few dollars and they come after you with relentless fervor.

NYPD is just another city gang, except they carry a badge. To them everyone is guilty. I was walking down Roosevelt Avenue after going to the bank. I took out $60 to pay Banco Popular in the morning; that was my plan. I used to pay my credit card on the first Saturday of the month. My intention was to visit a friend who owned a bodega on Eighty-Fifth Street and Roosevelt Avenue. When I began to cross Eighty-Fourth Street, a car pulled up in front of me, and a little guy grabbed me. I pushed him to the floor, not knowing who he was. Then a giant of a man got out of the driver's side of the car and said, "Put your hands on the car." This was when I realized they were cops. The little guy cuffed me real tight, cutting the circulation to my hands, and placed me in a paddy wagon. I was the first one to be arrested in an ongoing sweep by the police that night. Grabbing anyone that was walking in the area.

They took me out several times and asked to read a few signs, always looking at the elevated subway, the number 7 line. I believe they were trying to ID me. Later I overheard the undercover detective say to a white-shirt supervisor, "We don't think this is the guy." The white-shirt replied, "Fuck him, put him through the system." That's just how they operate. I later had to spend $10,000 and take a bunch of annual leave to clear my name. This is why I know that not everyone that's locked up in Rikers is guilty. I used to respect the police. I can't stand them now.

Rikers Island, you could talk about this place for a week and would only scratch the surface, of the complexity of this jailhouse. When they first started to put cameras in all sorts of areas in the jail, I knew this would become a major problem for the corrections department. Superiors were tickled pink. They would be able to better monitor their personnel and inmates. What was to be a new tool of enforcement quickly turned into a nightmare. Rikers Island is now out of control with no relief in sight. This camera installation created a lawsuit monster that is still having negative ramifications to this date.

Inmates are no longer fearful of the corrections officer. In fact they'll challenge them to do something so as to catch them on camera.

CHAPTER 31

When I first met Julio Gonzalez, the guy who burned down the Happy Land Club in the South Bronx, killing eighty-nine partygoers, incinerating them to death, he was mercilessly beaten every day anywhere by the corrections officers who were assigned to protect him. If there had been cameras back then, this would have never happened. You see, these people place themselves above the law. They become judge, jury, and executioner. That's not what they signed up for; their job is to protect.

At the time that Julio Gonzalez burned down the Happy Land Club, killing eighty-nine partygoers, he was in his right mind. Pablo Escobar, the cocaine drug lord at the time who was worth $7 billion, placed a million-dollar bounty on his head. A small amount for this guy. He wanted him dead. All of the people who died in this inferno were Latinos. He was pissed off, and revenge was on his mind. But the corrections department couldn't allow this assassination to take place. Every resource had to be utilized to ensure proper transportation from one place to another without incident. They used three corrections vans to disguise their destination!

Julio came looking for his girlfriend at the Happy Land Club after he was told by her, "I don't love you anymore. Please get out."

He couldn't accept this ultimatum. He decided to go looking for an alternative to his problem. He waited for the bus. It didn't come for a long time. He decided to walk home.

He went past a garbage-filled empty lot when he spotted a Prestone antifreeze canister. He went to a gas station and bought a gallon of gas. He then walked back to the club and poured it all over the front door and lit a match. He wandered aimlessly around the area for approximately an hour before returning to the scene of the crime. By now the fire department were stacking the bodies on the sidewalk, eighty-nine in total. The most horrific killing in the history of New York City. Everyone was shocked by these murders. After his arrest, he was quickly transported to Bellevue for a psychiatric evaluation. As part of the treatment team, I was in direct contact with this animal. But we had to view him as a patient. You are not allowed to pass judgment. It was very difficult to be impartial, and I was new to this concept.

When I walked into Julio Gonzalez's housing cell, I had to put my arms spread eagle against the wall, like a Christ figure. Security was in high alert due to the bounty placed on Julio's head by Pablo Escobar, the cocaine kingpin of Columbia.

"How are you doing, Mr. Gonzalez?" I asked. He was a Cuban refugee who had jumped on a boat headed for America with nothing to lose.

"I'm all right," he stated. "I want to let everybody know, I didn't mean to kill all those people." He was remorseful and stated, "I was drunk and out of my mind." He said, "I'm so embarrassed, the whole city's talking about me, that I'm a monster." He wanted everyone to know, "I'm not crazy. Please tell them. Please, please, tell them, I'm not crazy. I didn't mean to hurt anybody. It was an accident." He said this over and over again, trying to convince me and perhaps the whole city that he didn't intentionally kill those people.

I told him, "You have to tell that to the judge and the jury and mount your defense in court."

He looked haggard, as though he hadn't slept in a while. He had just been arrested four days ago, and things we're beginning to sink in. His eyes swelled, and he began to cry. I told him, "Crying is not going to help. You have to make preparations to get yourself together and defend yourself against these charges."

He placed folded hands on top of his head, got up from the bed, and began to pace around the room. "What the fuck did I do?" he shouted. He was still crying and began to bang his head against the wall. "Stop! Stop!" I yelled at him. He was on a suicide watch by both the medical and correctional staff. They ran into the room and grabbed ahold of him to prevent any further damage. In a few moments the whole staff was in his room. They needed to give him an injection and place him in restraints.

Dr. Levine was now talking to him. "Mr. Gonzalez, we can't allow you to hurt yourself. Do you understand?"

Dr. Levine ordered that Julio would be given five milligrams of Haldol, two milligrams of Cogentin, and two milligrams of Ativan.

Dr.Levine asked his staff to meet up in the conference room. "What happened, Rubildo? Tell me you didn't agitate this patient," he asked me in an irritated voice.

"Listen, Levine, I just did what you told me to do," I said. These high-profile cases were always a problem for the staff. We were always under the microscope due in large part to the news media's relentless attempt to get inside information.

"So what kind of information did you collect?" Dr. Levine asked.

"I wasn't able to collect anything. He was crying and babbling on that it was an accident. Before I could react, he was banging his head against the wall," I told him.

I knew what Dr. Levine was trying to do. He was looking for a scapegoat. Someone he could blame if this patient severely injured himself. I was disappointed that he would place me in such a predicament. Over the years I was one of his confidants. A person he relied on to help keep order on the unit.

He told the staff, "We need to move this guy out as soon as possible. He doesn't appear to be under any major distress other than feeling remorseful." He lectured us on how to deal with this difficult patient. "We need to anticipate some of his acting-out behavior."

He then said, "Dr. Barkley and myself will be doing the 730 psych evaluation tomorrow morning."

Early the next day, Dr.Levine had Mr. Gonzalez brought into the interview room, where they proceeded to rush through the 730 psych evaluation. By two thirty that afternoon, after being found fit to stand trial, Mr. Gonzalez was headed back to Rikers Island. He never returned to our facility.

After tension subsided, Dr.Levine called me into his office and apologized for making me the focal point of the incident the day before. "I'm sorry for calling you out yesterday," he said. I told him, "Not a problem, I understand you were under a lot of stress." I accepted his apology, but now I was aware that anyone could be thrown under the bus. I had a lot of respect for Dr. Levine, but now I didn't trust him. I never told him how I felt in order to avoid creating a rift between us. But our relationship had changed.

It cost hundreds of dollars to safeguard this individual while in the custody of corrections or while in the hospital. No one wants to lose a prisoner that you are responsible to protect; heads would roll if that ever happened. Another inmate, Davis, had a gun battle with a few cops in the Bronx. The Bronx was hot back then. He killed two and wounded three. Corrections was dying to give him their justice. An old-fashioned beating that they were experts at delivering, no facial bruises or broken bones. I began to consume large amounts of cocaine and alcohol to kill the pain of working with these degenerates.

CHAPTER 32

But I can tell you from past experiences that Rikers Island has some of the most talented guys on the planet, hands down. Presently there are two or three guys that could play in the NBA. There are poets, painters, songwriters. You name it, there is someone who is locked up who can do it to the max, and that's the sad part. That these gifted individuals are rotting away in some cell, not only here in Rikers Island, but across the country. Give these guys a chemistry set, a lab coat and they will find the cure for cancer. But that's the thing about jail and prison; it makes everybody equal, but having a talent may give you a small edge to survive. If you are able to sketch a face, you can use it to barter, make something out of nothing. The most sought-after dudes in jail are your jailhouse lawyers. These guys can write a court brief in a nanosecond, and they know the penal code like the back of their hand. They are the ones that are most in demand.

People pay big bucks for this ability. Individuals who are unable to make bail have no choice but to fight their case from behind bars. And if you are assigned legal aid by the courts or an 18-b lawyer, they don't have your best interests in mind. You must research. Your research is crucial when you are poor and indigent because no one is going to stick up for you. All these assigned lawyers just want to make a deal to clear their docket, not in your best interest.

CHAPTER 33

I was devastated when my close friend Maurice Robinson passed away. We both came to Bellevue at the same time, December 31, 1979, and quickly became cohorts. He would come to my house for Super Bowl Sunday, NBA finals, or just to hang out in the backyard. He was a special guy.

One day Mo came up to me and asked, "Are you dealing coke?" I was stunned by his candor, but that was Mo. He always gave it to you straight. He told me there was a guy who would be willing to purchase a large quantity. That we could make a bundle of cash and he was reliable. I was always paranoid about anyone I didn't know, but if Mo made a recommendation, I would have to look into his boy.

This guy wanted to buy a kilo right off the bat. That made me leery and uncomfortable. In this business, you can't trust anyone. If you get busted for a kilo, that costs $19,000, you are facing fifteen years.

Mo was a nursing assistant making $22,000 a year before taxes, with a growing family. Hell, the kilo he wanted to buy with his buddy cost just $3,000 less than his gross salary. What can you do with $22,000? He wanted to make a few dollars and get out quickly, but that's not how human nature operates. Once people get a taste of money, you're done. It's a thirst not easily quenched. You keep coming back for more.

And sure enough, Mo dove headfirst into the trade. My supplier was Roberto, the husband of Ana Escobar, the woman to whom I had given the leather coat. He came to the States a few years later and started to run the business.

The first kilo of cocaine I ever sold took place in Burger Fest, on Astoria Boulevard and 92nd Street. I was scared out of my mind. My heart was pumping. The thought of getting caught just wouldn't go away. The adrenaline racing through my bloodstream made me lightheaded. In this situation I was not in control; it made me uneasy. After the transaction was done, Roberto gave me $300. I asked, "What the fuck is this shit?" He told me that was my commission. "You make a $19,000 transaction and I get $300. Are you crazy!"

Why would I take such a big risk? I sold a gram of coke and made $50. I never went back to getting involved in the sale of large quantities of coke as the payoff was not worth it for me. I am sure Roberto made a killing in that deal.

CHAPTER 34

In the meantime at Rikers Island, corruption was widespread. Corrections officers were being busted on a monthly basis for one thing or another. The main culprit was the smuggling of contraband into the institution. This activity was rampant with these yo-yos, whether drugs, alcohol, tobacco, razor blades, or even a loaded gun ready for use. A female officer who had fallen in love with an inmate brought him a loaded gun so he could settle a score with one of his peers. It's mind-boggling that these individuals have such big egos to think they will succeed where so many others have failed. The list goes on and on but not limited to corrections officers. Civilians are in this game also. Nurses, supervisors, and drug counselors have all been arrested and charged with felonies that carry a minimum of seven years in prison. Individuals with ten, fifteen, and twenty years on the job make a nice income, yet many have been terminated on the spot for these indiscretions.

Jason Rodriguez was a drug counselor running a unit that housed forty men with substance-abuse pathologies. He also worked at a hospital in a similar capacity, making pretty good money. He will not become a millionaire but made enough money to own his own home and car and take an occasional vacation, or he would splurge on his grandchildren.

Jason Rodriguez, the drug counselor, had a lot of physical problems. He was a grumpy old guy who walked with a limp and needed a cane to help him get around. His hair was always tied up in a ponytail, a sign that he was part of the hippie culture years ago.

"Rubildo!" he shouted while walking down the massive hallways of Rikers Island at C 95 jail. "Let's do lunch!" he said. I was trying to stay away from him by now. Afraid that our friendship would make me guilty by association by all the staff. I didn't need a problem like him at this point in my career.

"Jay, I am busy, I can't step out right now," I told him.

"Lately you've been avoiding me. Why?" he asked while trying to catch up to me.

I stopped and waited for him. I knew he was in pain. "I'm not trying to avoid you, I'm just busy," I said to him.

"How about the unit, you haven't been there in months," he asked.

"It has nothing to do with you, I just lost interest in working there anymore," I told him. I didn't like this type of probing that he was doing to me. I was trying not to lose my cool. He had a tendency to get under people's skin with his crude mannerism. He was always arguing and badgering corrections staff; he hated them.

"Aren't you supposed to be helping me with this program?" he asked in a coarse attitude.

"No!" I shot back. "When Dr. Grant first started this program, he asked me, Mr. Johnson, and Mr. Brown to volunteer some time on that service," I told him. "It was not mandatory for me to be on that service," I continued to explain to him. "I don't understand why we are discussing this in the middle of this hallway," I said. "If you want to discuss this any further, meet me in my office."

He looked at me with hate in his eyes. "Let's go there now," he said.

I didn't say anything else while we walked to S mod, where my office was located. When we got there, I took my coat off and placed it on a hanger, threw my hat on a chair, and sat down. I could see he was angry at me, but I didn't care. He had no business trying to tell me what to do. I was not his staff member.

"What is your problem?" he asked.

"Listen, Jay, I don't want to say something that would hurt you or offend you, but I have no interest in working with you anymore," I said.

"What did I do?" he asked with a coy smile on his face.

"I just don't think we're on the same page on how this program should be run," I told him. "So what would you do different? How could the program be improved?" he asked.

The program was for low-level drug dealers and abusers looking to get into outside drug treatment programs, an alternative to incarceration. Jason's job was to find these individuals long-term rehabilitation facilities. He had been a heroin addict for a long time so he had a good working knowledge about this format. He was doing pretty well until he started to use again. That was his downfall.

"The program is not the problem, the problem is you," I told him in a stern voice. He looked in shock when I told him that. He couldn't make eye contact, a sign he knew he had been exposed. He slumped over on the chair, looking defeated. All the energy was sapped out of his body. He felt crushed by my assessment. "I've been reading body language for nearly forty years. You can't tell me that you don't have a problem," I told him.

On occasion I would go to lunch with this guy and help him run the program. But I saw his mood had changed dramatically. I knew he began to use again. If you are sitting in your office in the middle of February with the windows open, dressed in a T-shirt, the fan blowing, and you're nodding out, you have a problem. I knew I had to stay away from this guy.

Not long after that, a patient/inmate went into a convulsion. He had overdosed on a few bags of heroin. While he was being medically treated, a bag of dope fell out of his pocket. A captain was called in to investigate. Remember, an infraction of this type carries an additional seven-year sentence. There were posters plastered all over the jail with a warning about this, and everybody knew. The patient/inmate gave up Jason right away. This was reported to the police, which began an investigation into Jason's activities. They found out he would leave his house at five o'clock in the morning. After making a quick stop a few miles from his place, he would head to Rikers. One morning he was stopped by the police and searched. They found ten bundles of dope on his person. That's one hundred bags of heroin.

When he got busted bringing in ten bundles of heroin into Rikers Island, nobody was shocked. Everyone was aware that he had been arrested before for drug possession. Heroin addiction has a lot of demons trying to trigger your mind. Few individuals could survive this madness.

When he got arrested, the first individual he wanted to talk to was me. I spoke with Ms. Sanders, our unit chief, concerning this matter. She asked me, "What do you want to do?"

I told her, "I really don't want to be involved with this guy. There's gonna be a stigma attached to me because of his actions."

She said, "I will inform the corrections department that you're not interested in meeting with this guy."

He had been brought into C 95 after being arrested, the same jail he worked as a drug counselor. You call that irony.

Sure enough, correction officers were making fun of me, asking me, "How's your buddy Rodriguez?" I gave them the middle finger and said, "I don't have friends that get high." The fact is that I didn't have male friends. I never had a need for them; women were my partners. They always treated me with respect. It was easy to talk to them;

they were always nurturing me. I loved it. What is it about them? I think it is their breasts. I could look them in the eye and feel better.

It took several years before that abuse finally died down. I never saw him again or cared to see him. For a long period of time I was made fun of because of that motherfucker.

CHAPTER 35

I wish I could tell you that this was an isolated incident or poor judgment by a few individuals. But the reality is that on a monthly basis staff is being handcuffed and dragged into court on felony charges.

There are deviant sexual encounters taking place all over Rikers Island. Female corrections officers are getting pregnant by inmates. They're doing it in offices, stairwells, parking lots, wherever possible. Whatever happened to a motel room? No one can spring a few bucks for privacy anymore.

That's the culture that permeates throughout this facility. It's like the Mafia; if you can't kill the head, you can't kill the body. So as long as new recruits arrive, some are going to think they could get away with something. They have a full lproof gimmick to get away.

Bellevue Hospital is no different. You would think a hospital's personnel should have a higher standard. The whole atmosphere at Rikers Island is geared to promote depression. A sane person would never adjust to this lack of quality of life. Nothing good comes out of being there. The food is the first thing you notice; it smells like the garbage truck that goes past your house in the morning. There is no privacy. The inmates smell like shit. Some in the mental observation area go as far as smearing themselves with crap to avoid facing their charges, what we call malingering or playing crazy. But if they go that far, the medical profession cannot ignore these gestures. Their licenses are on the line, so rather than take a chance, they send them to Bellevue Hospital to be stabilized through chemical intervention.

Bellevue Hospital, due to its landmark status, can't be financially run into the ground although many administrators in the past have tried. If Bellevue were a private company, it would have gone into bankruptcy decades ago. But Bellevue has a golden parachute that secures it with financial stability for centuries to come, the city of New York.

Not long ago a coordinating manager administrator told me custom-made beds were ordered. When they arrived, they didn't fit properly. This was not a problem for Bellevue. They just reordered another set of beds. The original set of beds now sits in a subbasement of the hospital, rotting away. This is the norm, not the exception. Throughout this great institution, similar mistakes are taking place at an alarming rate with no consequences or accountability. It hurts me that these sycophants with no leadership qualities are in charge of this beautiful palace.

Bellevue is the flagship hospital of Health and Hospitals Corporation, founded in March 31, 1736. It is the most recognizable hospital on the planet. Most New Yorkers don't even know its address, but they know where it's located. There's an old Mexican saying that when administration is thrown out of power, Jesus Christ falls from the cross because even the nails are stolen. That's the sort of corruption that took place after Hurricane Sandy at Bellevue. Everything was taken.

CHAPTER 36

It was difficult to face these individuals I was working with without having feelings of guilt. After a while I didn't give a fuck. I decided that Bellevue had plenty of people that needed to borrow money. My first customer was Kathy Diaz. She was a single mom raising two daughters and struggling to make ends meet on her nurse's aide salary. She would routinely come up to me and ask, "Rubildo, can I borrow $20?" The following paycheck, she would give me twenty bucks and say, "Thanks for helping me out."

I made a proposition to her. I told her, "I'll give you $1,000, and you pay me back $100 each pay period for thirteen paychecks." She jumped at the opportunity to have that kind of money in her hand all at once. People only see the short-term benefits of being in debt to a loan shark. I told her, "Be careful how you manage this money. It is not a long-term solution for your financial problems."

She said, "Don't worry, I got you."

I calculated that it would take six months and two weeks for her to pay me back the full amount. My major concern was whether allocating $1,000 for $300 return would be beneficial for me. I had researched other loan sharks doing business at Bellevue, and they told me that was the going rate, $300 return on $1,000 investment. They also told me I should raise the vig from $100 to maybe $200 every paycheck to cut the time in half.

It turned out that my investment in Mrs. Diaz would pay dividends in other ways. She brought in a customer who wanted to borrow $500 within a few days. She wanted to know what would be her commission. "If I bring you customers, how much would I get paid?" she asked. This was a new angle in my business dealings. I wasn't sure how to respond to her question. I told her, "Give me a few days to think about it, and I'll get right back to you."

When I spoke to her later, I told her, "I don't want to know your customers, they are your responsibility. If they don't pay, you have to come up with the money. Are you willing to accept those terms?"

She looked somewhat puzzled, fearful that she might be victimized by one of her customers. "Listen, Rubildo," she said, "I don't want to take that kind of chance."

I responded by giving her a lecture on business etiquette. "You can't have your cake and eat it too." I told her, "Keep the loans low to begin with, this way you could minimize your losses."

She appeared nervous, unable to decide whether to plunge into this kind of business. Your average person never feels comfortable getting involved with the unknown.

She brought me her first customer, a desperate single mom who needed $500. Her rent was due.

She then asked me, "How much am I going to make on this transaction?"

I then told her, "I will give you $25 at the back end of the transaction."

She objected to my deal. "I need more money than that, I'm taking a big chance for a few dollars," she said.

"I'm the one that's taking a risk," I told her. "It's my money that is involved." She wanted to manipulate the situation to her benefit, and I was not buying that. "Listen," I told her, "just forget it, just pay me my money every paycheck, and we'll be all right." But she didn't want to let it go. She wanted to be part of this business. "It's okay, give me a chance to make some money," she said, begging me to help her anyway I could.

She went around looking for several more customers. By now, after a few weeks, she had seven new additions to the growing list of customers. I was impressed with her versatility. I told her again, "I don't want to know your customers." She kept everything a big secret. No one would know that we were doing business together.

We were constantly on the cell phone talking about our business transactions. She then, out of nowhere, asked me for a loan without interest payment. I told her, "No!" She wanted to borrow $5,000 without an interest payment.

She claimed, "I want to buy a house in Santo Domingo."

I told her, "I don't care if you want to buy an igloo in the Yukon wilderness, I'm not going to lend you that kind of money." I could see she was upset, but the subject matter was never broached again.

CHAPTER 37

The Gang's organizations reach beyond the walls of Rikers Island. They're capable of extorting whole families on the outside. Initially they ask you nicely, "Can you give me a call? I like your sneakers." Do yourself a favor; don't turn them down. They will take it by force anyway. That's their modus operandi. Anything that they see and want, they take. If you protest, you'll get a beaten; it's that simple. But if they get their tentacles into your family, it turns into a never-ending nightmare for everyone involved.

The world really changed after September 11, 2001. Although New Yorkers are a tough breed, they nevertheless feared the next possible catastrophe. Could it be possible that a small nuclear device be walked into our great city and detonated, destroying every facet of our great city, the Statue of Liberty, the Empire State Building, the Brooklyn Bridge? A culture that brought us ragtime, jazz, rhythm and blues, and hip-hop, the artistic mecca of our time evaporating in a nuclear cloud.

Before 9/11 the New York City population had a substance-abuse problem of 18 to 22 percent. After the bombing, it shot up to 24 to 26 percent. These are epidemic numbers. The government has to intervene.

Bellevue personnel had always had a substance abuse problem. Back in 1987, twenty-three people were arrested as a drug enterprise in the basement of this great building. Another guy was busted with two kilos of cocaine and a loaded Glock in his locker. There's no big mystery here. Five thousand people work at Bellevue, and some of them are drug dealers, including myself.

If you hang out in the hallways of Bellevue Hospital long enough someone is going to come up to you and ask, "Are you looking for something?" Nearly 70 percent of Bellevue staff makes a yearly income of $35,00 to $45,000. Studio apartments are renting for $2,000 to $2,200 a month. Many of them can't afford this extravagant rent. One-third of the New York City shelter population are working people. I have correction officers with a base salary of $82,000 asking for loans. I walked into a convenience store to buy a jar of mayonnaise and a container of milk; it cost me $13. When I complained to the clerk, he told me go to the supermarket, they have better prices. I remember shopping with my mother and bringing three to four bags of groceries for $13.

My business continued to explode. Someone warned me to be careful; they wanted to rip me off, rob me. Everyone knew I always carried a large amount of cash after payday. I bought a gun. I carried a fully loaded Glock, prepared to use it at any time. If someone tried to hurt me, I would unload on them without remorse. I didn't give a fuck. I knew it was dangerous to carry large amounts of money at any time in Bellevue Hospital. I had been looking over my shoulders for a long time. Bellevue was full of thugs ready to pounce on anyone who failed to be vigilant.

A pair of Air Jordans costs well over $100. People with large expendable incomes are not buying these fancy sneakers; they can't afford them. Walk into any ghetto in the United States, and every adolescent male is wearing these overpriced sneakers. Some of the adolescents have one hundred to two hundred pairs of these sneakers. They are a status symbol created by large conglomerates such as Nike. It's insane how our priorities have changed in the past thirty years. Adolescents have killed for these sneakers. What motivates an individual to kill someone for a pair of sneakers? I often thought about the religious doctrines the Catholic Church had provided me with and whether they apply to my upbringing. I had a Glock in my hand ready to use if someone tried to harm me and that was not part of the church's teachings. But the best weapon in your arsenal is always feel comfortable in your own skin. If you look in the mirror and see a great guy, he'll always be there. There's no morality in Bellevue Hospital. Everyone is trying to get over on someone. And I understand that. When the World Trade Center was bombed by airplanes, I was in a suite listening on a radio. At first I thought it was an accident.

The Federal government gave Bellevue a gazillion dollars to stem the tide of addiction after 9/11. If you place a police roadblock at any exit, 25 percent of the vehicles stopped will be found drinking and drugging or under the influence of drugs and alcohol. This is a staggering number. Can you imagine one out of four vehicles driving by you can kill you? Sometimes I sit in my backyard looking at the birds; they have a system of corruption also. There's a constant competition for the bread I throw back there. He who eats the fastest eats the most. That's the reality.

When Puerto Ricans were given the opportunity to handle the cash, they became corrupt also. Even some of the first Puerto Rican politicians sold their souls to the devil. It's a given to always follow the money. Small-scale or large-scale corruption, it's no different.

But I was no fool. You wanted to borrow money, you had to pay the interest.

CHAPTER 38

I ran into Wanda Smith at Citibank. She had curly red hair and was doing an internship at Bellevue Hospital forensic unit. Whenever she worked on the service, she had to wear a lab coat. She would wear her pants so tight you could see her panty lines, and it would drive our patients wild. She was a little flirtatious and enjoyed the attention she was getting from our patients. I was making a cash deposit to my business and saw an opportunity to approach her about this behavior.

"Ms. Smith, how are you doing?" I asked.

"Oh, Mr. Rubildo, how's my favorite therapist?" she said.

"I would like to discuss something with you, but I hope you don't get offended," I told her.

"Tell me, what is it? I won't be offended, I could handle this," she said.

"You've been working on our service for a few months now, and you are a very attractive woman," I told her. "With this population, you have to be careful how you dress."

She then said, "I'm not dressing for the population, I'm dressing for you, and I'm glad you noticed me." I was left speechless by her comment. "You're a handsome man, and I would like to be with you," she continued to verbalize her feelings. "Why don't we go to your office, and I'll show you a good time," she said without hesitation.

All the blood in my body rushed to my face. I felt flush, warm around my neck area. I was temporarily paralyzed, unable to move. It took me about twenty seconds to regain my composure. Finally I asked, "Why me?"

She responded to my question with a question. "Why not you?"

I said to her, "Well, I'm part of the treatment team helping to educate you on how to work with this population, there may be a conflict of interest."

She told me, "I've been trying to talk to you since I got here a few months back. I know how to keep quiet, trust me." She continued to provide reasons why we should get together "I'm a big girl, you don't have to worry about me talking to anyone about us."

I told her, "What the hell, let's do this, but not in my office."

She moved her five-foot-seven-inch, 125-pound figure close to me and said, "You will not regret this."

I told her, "I'll make plans. We'll meet somewhere outside of Bellevue."

We both completed our banking transactions and said good-bye. As she walked away, I continued to look at her ass. It was beautiful.

The next day we had lunch together, and she asked me, "Have you made any arrangements?"

I suggested to her, "Let's go to a nearby hotel."

She nodded her head in agreement and asked, "Is four o'clock all right with you?"

I responded in the affirmative, "Yes." Four o'clock was the time I headed toward Rikers Island. But today I would be using emergency annual leave as an excuse not to go work. Being able to fuck a twenty-five-year-old redhead was one of my fantasies. I couldn't pass this up. I wanted to know if her pubic hairs matched the long curly red mane she had on top of her head.

We walked to a five-star hotel located on Thirty-Second Street between Fifth and Sixth Avenue in midtown Manhattan. I've walked through that area hundreds of times but never knew a five-star hotel was there. New York City is a fantastic cultural mecca. You can find the best places in the world right around the corner. Once I was wandering around Tenth Street and First Avenue when I walked into a jazz club and had the best time of my life.

It was mid-June. The heat was unbearable, and I had this fantastic-looking girl wrapped around my arm, looking for a place to get fucked.

I bought a bottle of frozen champagne at Thirtieth Street and Third Avenue, hoping it would stay cold by the time we got there. I had ordered it the day before in order to ensure it would stay cold for our rendezvous. I didn't leave anything to chance when it came to making love with women. I wanted to give them the best time of their lives. That was my style.

On our way there, I asked her, "Do you have condoms?"

She said, "We are going raw, baby. You don't need no stinking condoms. I take the pill." This girl was beginning to scare me. I felt like she was trying to set me up. It was too perfect.

When we got to the hotel, she let me pay and ran upstairs with the card to enter the room. It took me a few minutes to check in, but she was already upstairs. I decided to take the elevator to the second floor instead of walking up. I knocked on the door instead of using my card. I was curious to see what she looked like. She yelled at the top of her lungs, "Hold on, I'll be right there." When she pulled open the door, all she had on were red panties and a bra. I was ecstatic that she had given me this opportunity to fuck her. When I looked at her pussy, she had red pubic hair. I turned her around and sucked her ass, which also had a few red pubic hairs. I pulled out the champagne bottle, which was still cold, and three and a half grams of cocaine. She screamed out loud, "I knew you got high!" We snorted for the next four hours. She loved it.

She tried to talk to me, but I was too fucked up to listen. I told her, "Just calm down and relax."

She left our unit a month later and called me numerous times. On a few occasions we met up for lunch, and we ran into the five-star hotel she loved.

CHAPTER 39

Later I found out she became a cocaine whore. I hope it wasn't my fault.

When you're in the business of selling jewelry, cocaine and lending money, women gravitate to you like you're a supermagnet. One girl told me, "I don't want to break up your marriage. I just want to fuck you. You are a good looking guy. You dress well, you're smart, and you smell good. You're the kind of man I would love to be with. To rip your ass apart is my pleasure." I had to be careful not to fall for this kind of line. Eventually you'll pay for it somewhere down the road. "My baby needs a pair of sneakers" or "I'm short with my rent this month," the list will grow and grow and grow, but I wasn't having any of that. You buy jewelry, you buy cocaine, you borrow money, you have to pay. Everyone is the same. You can't have any favorites. In Bellevue there are also many women who can barely make ends meet, desperados who sell their bodies at the drop of a dime if that's what it takes.

I get it, single mom raising one or two children by herself, making $37,000 a year. It's hard to make ends meet standing at the edge of being homeless. If I were in the same predicament, I would sell my body also. For many of these desperate women, their pussy is the only asset they have, so why not use it for groceries? Women would tell me I had a sexual aura. They were always trying to pick me up, I knew it was because of the money. But I was no fool. You wanted to borrow money, you had to pay the interest. There was no exception to this rule, a piece of ass I could get anywhere, making money was difficult and I did not want to violate my homefront.

I always had a soft spot for single moms. You look into their faces and there's a sense of hopelessness that can't be denied. Not them, but the children who depend on their mother's resilience to work it out. To get it done. It breaks my heart to think a mother would sell her ass for her child. I blame those dumb motherfuckers who refuse to be responsible for their actions. Fathers are the supreme figure in the nuclear family.

My son and daughters thought I was a god when they were growing up. It was a special pleasure being there for them when they needed me most. Why would a father abandon his child at this time?

My grandfather grew sugarcane for the United States government, so I have a history in business. It's in my DNA, part of my wealth-making process.

Thirty years ago I was criticized for stating that the biggest problem at Rikers Island was the lack of a father figure. Later Steve Harvey was also castigated for making similar statements. If there's no parental guidance to help your child navigate the obstacles of society, then your child is going to have problems.

To this day I can still hear my father's voice telling me to be careful. I thought he was such an idiot at the time. I hated everything about him. The fact that he spoke in broken English embarrassed me. The music he played, salsa, I couldn't stand it. Today that's the only music that I play in my car. He wore suspenders, ties, suits, colognes, hats, and now I'm the spitting image of my dad, not a bad thing, but when I was eighteen years old, I hated him with a passion. It took me a while to accept the fact that he was a genius helping me understand life. I wish that he was here today so I could tell him that, but he's long gone.

My mother was a special creature. She always had her claws out to kill a prey. She taught me to be ruthless. I get my business savvy from them. My father and mother ran a cockfighting ring. They had grocery stores, which they call bodegas today. They owned buildings in the Lower East Side, which today are worth millions of dollars. My beautiful aunt and I spent endless hours together eating sugarcane. She thought I was her personal doll.

CHAPTER 40

I'm shocked that Bellevue Hospital's present administration remained intact. That after all this corruptive activity, the Bloomberg and de Blasio hierarchy would allow this kind of indifference to function without impunity. Again it shows the resilience of the spirit of Bellevue, that despite the corruptive nature of people, it survives. Since 1736 it has been the public health provider, the first of its kind, for all of New York.

During a transit strike, I was mandated to stay at Bellevue as a support staff. I was elated to spend a few days at this great institution and be paid overtime. I walked around the area, and I was in awe of the magnificence of this great creation. A place where poor or rich can be treated for their afflictions without question. But that's the beauty of Bellevue.

You can't kill Bellevue, and anyone who works there is privy to this idea. We are always complaining about something. We are not happy; we don't get paid enough. But if you are working here, you must be crazy. When I was floated to Jacobi Hospital soon after Hurricane Sandy, I was devastated. I didn't want to be there. Bellevue was my home for over thirty-three years, and I felt lost. All my customers were scattered to every corner of the city. I was unable to collect any money. My income disappeared overnight. I had grown accustomed to a certain lifestyle, and now I had to keep an eye on how I used my money. No more Atlantic City for me or hanging in the bars blowing $100 or $200 on entertainment whenever I wanted. These new restraints were difficult for me because it also exposed the frailty of my finances. How easily things could change from one moment to the next. I became angry at myself for the financial predicament I found myself in at that time. If I called someone about their debt, they all said the same thing, "I'll see you when you get back." It was like they rehearsed together. I planned to punish every one of them for playing me this way. I was delusional, angry. I blamed my customers for Hurricane Sandy. But soon after we got back, three months later, everything was forgiven. You have to understand, I was making $10,000 to $15,000 a month extra. Now I had to depend on income from my jobs, a miserable $4,400 a month. Initially I was in shock, but I knew that the great institution of Bellevue would be up and running soon. When you talk about corruption all city agencies have a similar affliction, a never-ending search on how to best steal money. Rikers Island is no different. They treat these agencies like piggy banks. The closer you get to the money, the easier it is to take it.

CHAPTER 41

Visit Officer Ramos at Rikers Island was presented with a sweet deal by inmate Vera. For $300 a visit he would allow inmate Vera to smuggle drugs into the facility. In addition, Mr. Vera's wife would wait for the officer at the other side of the Rikers Island Bridge. They would go to a motel, have sex, and the transaction was completed. This went on for a couple of months without incident. But for this greedy motherfucker, $300 wasn't enough. He upped his price to $500 in addition to having sex in the motel room. Mr. Vera asked to see a captain, and an investigation was launched into Officer Ramos's dealings. They set up Officer Ramos.

Officer Ramos violated two major commandments of thievery, excessive greed, and making deals with inmates. This is why I've never developed a crew. It creates too many variables, and you can be easily inculpated by a disgruntled worker willing to save their own skin. If I'm going to take a fall, it's going to be because of my own stupidity. Loyalty is a bygone mantra in an era that has expired.

The few times I spoke to Officer Ramos, he claimed, "Rubildo, you can't trust these motherfuckers. They'll stab you in the back in a minute."

I told him, "I was pulled over by a corrections officer the first day on the job thirty-six years ago. He warned me never to make deals with any of these guys, it'll come back to bite you in the ass. I heeded his warning my whole career."

Ironically, a few weeks after giving me a big speech about not trusting inmates, Officer Ramos was handcuffed at his regular post in front of everybody and immediately transferred to Sing Sing prison. Any officer arrested for criminal activity in the Rikers Island facility is sent to Sing Sing prison, located at Westchester County, for protective reasons. They can't be housed in this area for obvious reasons; their lives would be in danger. It was later learned by intelligence gathering that Officer Ramos was allowing cellphones to be smuggled into the jail. Here was an eighteen-year veteran with two years to go before retiring with a huge pension who couldn't control his greed. This is just the tip of the iceberg. What he has done over the years, who knows.

Mr. Vera made a deal to get his sentence reduced. Once they get their claws in you, it's over. These are not rookies. These are veterans with ten to fifteen years on the job. Money has that sort of seduction that no one can ignore it.

You could hear Corrections Officer Daniel Bryant yelling one hundred yards away, "We are in alarm status, there will be no movement by civilian staff or inmates." He was an irascible old soldier who hated clinicians with a passion. An old-school paramilitary personnel who felt threatened by the medical changes that were taking place around him. The corrections department is a weird breed. They always want to be in control. On a daily basis there are alarms going off. This means that somewhere in the facility there is a problem. So all movement must stop during this period of time. It's an odd system they have developed to contain violence. It doesn't matter whether this archaic or obsolete way of doing things is not working. We are in control and that's corrections format.

I met CO Dennis twenty-five years ago when he was a young whippersnapper ready to enforce the law at all costs. We've had a long history together, bumping heads about prison rights. We would converse for long periods of time about prison rights. He would never back down, stating, "If they are here, they did something fucking wrong, you can't convince me otherwise, Ruboldo," as he called me. He would always mispronounce my name.

Over the years he grew bald, a little chubby around the waist, and his anger never diminished. When an alarm status is announced, you are not sure what happens. The only certainty you could surmise is that there has been some violent act committed somewhere in the facility. It could be a fight, a slashing, or even a kidnapping of a civilian staff member or a corrections officer. It could even be a riot in progress. A pro team is dispatched to the area where the incident occurred to extract the culprits. The whole place is shut down, and there will be no movement during this time.

Recently we've had a rash of kidnappings, and the whole jail gets tense during these periods. The uncertainty could be overbearing, and the stress level goes off the charts.

I asked Bryant while he was running around trying to secure all doors to the cafeteria, where we would be prisoners for the next twenty-five minutes, "What's going on, big guy?"

He shouted back, "They've taken a female corrections officer hostage at five quad lower, in the back of the building."

I asked him, "Do you know who it is?"

He said, "A rookie, she just started on the job. This jail is out of control." He stated in a subdued mood, "It's time for me to put my papers in. I'm going to retire."

Captain Rafferty was found dead of a heart attack two weeks after his retirement. It always diminishes my spirituality when you hear that a young man passed away. He was forty-two years old. He worked at Rikers Island for twenty years and never got a chance to collect his first pension check.

He was always hanging out in front of AMKC chain-smoking cigarettes and talking to anyone who would listen to him. I knew him for sixteen years, long before he became a captain. The stress they suffer is devastating.

He was an intense officer, always by the book. It really didn't surprise me when I heard he had died from a heart attack.

"Tell me something, Rubildo, what is this new mental health mentality you guys are trying to peddle off on us?" he asked in a commanding way.

He was an old-school type of guy who wouldn't take any guff from his staff or inmates. He didn't realize times were changing. Inmates had the upper hand now.

"Captain Rafferty, there's a new school of doing things with these patients, clients, detainees, inmates, whatever you want to call them. Your power has been negated," I told him. "There's a new world order when you deal with these guys nowadays." I was trying to be kind when I told him, "You are fucked."

For many of these old soldiers, time has passed them by. The days of beat-downs by corrections are over. But there still remains a cluster of individuals who have not received the latest memo with clear directives. Paramilitary personnel still thinking they could get away with physically abusing inmates.

New York City is drowning in official corruption. There's not one agency in the city in which someone wouldn't be willing to take a bribe.

Recently a corrections officer with nearly thirty years on the job was arrested for bringing contraband of tobacco and heroin into Rikers Island. This individual was making $82,000 in base salary per year. With a few days of overtime in a fifty-two-week period, he could get to earn over $130,000 a year.

He was in charge of the methadone line. Heroin addicts would be escorted by him to receive their daily poisonous dosage in a robotic state. All they wanted was to get a shot of synthetic heroin in order to relieve their pain.

He had a list of people who were dope sick.

Officer Garcia wanted to make money so he could enjoy a lavish lifestyle beyond his means.

According to investigative reports, he made $8,000 a year bringing contraband into Rikers Island over a twelve-year period. He was prolific in this business endeavor until someone broke the con code and ratted him out.

I had spoken with this officer many times. He hated the civilian staff. He was a short irascible man with a Napoleonic complex who spent most of the day screaming orders at inmates throughout the hallways.

"You know why I don't like you guys? Because you're always interfering with security. The clinical staff pampers these criminal monsters with bags of potato chips, underwear, T-shirts, what kind of crap is that? Do you really think this is going to change these people?" he said.

There was no sense in trying to explain to this old horse the concept of detainees. He wouldn't understand. But I hope by now he's being afforded the same rights he was trying to destroy as an officer.

This is the same guy who oversaw the methadone clinic and got the names of the inmates who were on the list. He would search them out to sell dime bags of heroin for $30. At his arraignment he told the judge, "Not guilty."

This was just another greedy, corrupt city personnel who thought the law didn't apply to him.

We are bombarded daily with statistics claiming 40 percent of the Rikers Island population has a mental illness. These are the most vulnerable clientele and they are taken advantage of by correction personnel.

MR. RUBILDO

Sometimes I sit in my backyard looking at the birds. They have a system of corruption also. There's a constant competition for the bread I throw back there. He who eats the fastest eats the most. That's the reality. My cocaine habit had ballooned out of control and gave me the delusion that I was functioning.

CHAPTER 42

Mrs. Yolanda Castro, the executive associate director of psychiatric nursing, had the audacity to start an agency for nursing and doctors at Bellevue Hospital. Imagine the benefits of running such an agency—no overhead, a string of nurses and doctors at your disposal, using Bellevue stationary to boot. One nurse in a five-day period can bring in to the agency $250. Now multiply that by one hundred nurses. You're talking about $25,000 in one month, not a bad profit. That's not counting the doctors who also made a nice pot of money for this corrupt agency that she unscrupulously managed. You have to understand this was not to staff Bellevue but all the city hospitals and private hospitals across the city. This was going on for years until a doctor complained about his money, and the whole scam was exposed.

These are the same individuals that were so concerned about me selling a $20 pair of earrings. If I had gotten caught selling anything at Bellevue, I would've been terminated on the spot. But these people have guardian angels. Mrs. Castro, instead of being arrested for her actions and given a significant amount of time in prison, was instead rewarded by being sent to be the executive associate director of psychiatric nursing at another high profile hospital which did not diminish her credibility at all. Her status remained intact.

ADNs (associate directors of nursing) were allowed to travel to the Philippines for six weeks at a time in order to recruit nurses. What a racket. They would get paid in full during this period of time recruiting nurses. What a joke.

There was a telephone line set up in my suite 19 West. You were allowed to make long-distance phone calls. There was a string of Filipinos lined up waiting to call their homeland. In one month they racked up over $1 million worth of calls. Nobody was held responsible for this. Just chalk it up to Bellevue's river of money. Luis Velez, the Executive Director of Bellevue Hospital, also was given an outlandish package of corruption. The soda vendors gave him a bribe of $600,000.00 under the table. He was arrested, posted bail and ran off to Santo Domingo. He was eventually extradited back to the United States where he made a deal with the Feds for no jail time. How could this be possible? If you rob a soda from one of these machines you are sent to Rikers for eight months. Bellevue has a special aura that cannot be explained and it continues to survive despite these poachers.

CHAPTER 43

Irina was an old, overweight, chain-smoking, wrinkle-faced babushka who worked as a nurse at Bellevue Hospital prison ward and wanted to kill her daughter-in-law, Stella. She had some beef with Stella, who was also a nurse at Bellevue Hospital. She was often floated to 19 W prison ward. Whenever Stella came to work on our unit, the first thing she did was take out a bottle of Benadryl and pour it into the patients' water canisters. She wanted to put people to sleep. Stella was a wild girl with a lot of problems, and Irina hated her with a passion.

Irina asked me, "If I ran Stella over with a car, would I be charged with murder?"

I was stunned to hear a health-care provider be so graphic about killing someone. She was an old-school Russian who had a distorted view about murder. She didn't give a fuck. Irina was obsessed with killing Stella.

"Irina," I said to her, "you're too old to be contemplating killing somebody. Do you want to spend the rest of your life locked up with a bunch of degenerates?"

She insisted, "If I can't see that little girl, Stella has to die."

Every time I came in contact with Irina, that's all she would talk about, killing Stella. In her mind, she thought this would solve the problem.

"Irina, you have to stop obsessing about Stella. It's going to get you in big trouble," I told her.

"But what can I do? She doesn't allow me to see my granddaughter. She's a horrible person," she said while tears began to swell in her eyes.

I told her, "Grandparents have rights also, but you have to go through the court system. You just can't take things into your own hands. This is a country of laws. You have a problem, you go to court."

I had to tell Irina, "Although we have a confidentiality privilege, if you continue to insist on hurting Stella, I would have to let the authorities know about your intent. I have a fiduciary duty to protect Stella."

She became incredulous. The thought of me ratting her out didn't sit well with her.

"Why are you siding with her?" she asked me.

"I don't give a fuck about you, Stella, or Victoria," I told her.

Irina was stubborn. She had no idea about the problem she was getting herself into with her sociopathic attitude. I had to disassociate myself from Irina in case she actually carried out her threat of eliminating the daughter-in-law.

Irina's grandchild was about two years old, and she would not allow her son, the father, to see her. This was what motivated Irina to have such feelings about Stella.

Victoria had blue eyes and curly blond hair. Irina was crazy about her. I told Irina, "I can't be involved in anything like this, murder is not my style. I don't even kill spiders in my house."

I never found out whether they worked things out between them. I stopped talking to Irina about murdering her daughter-in-law. It was not in my best interest, these shenanigans. There are hundreds of sociopaths like Irina working at Bellevue Hospital. Dozens are dismissed yearly for abusing patients, stealing, and insubordination.

Unfortunately, Bellevue has a bunch of these types of characters. Psychopaths willing to take outlandish risks with very little reward. Let's face it, Irina was a trained forensic psychiatry nurse. She knew the consequences. Why would she even contemplate doing something like murder?

CHAPTER 44

The underground economy, black market in Rikers Island, is carried out by trustees. Guys who sweep and mop the corridors, guys who transport the food across the whole institution, barbers, anyone who has a certain amount of freedom is employed by the gangs. Everything is run by gangs. They are in charge of all this activity. They are so resourceful, cunning, and versatile. To this day I still don't understand or know how they operate. And I'm privy to all of this information, but they don't allow me to get that close. I'm still an outsider in this world. Alcohol, marijuana, cocaine, heroin, and any other illicit drugs are transported by this group of guys. The main supplier of these contraband has to be correction officers or civilian staff. Somewhere along the line, they or we as a civilian staff must be involved in some capacity.

The slickest people on the planet are housed at Rikers Island. They always try to test me. They know I'm beyond reproach. I would never compromise my integrity for a few dollars, but they try tempting me on a constant basis. I've gotten so many offers for a pack of cigarettes, up to $100 for a pack of cigarettes. That's the way gangs work. They are relentless and keep offering me cash to see if I would succumb to their bullshit. The price will eventually make you give in. My response has always been, "If you can give me a job making $75,000 a year with benefits, then I'll give you a pack of cigarettes." I admire their ability to survive under adverse conditions. But I would never allow myself to be entangled in this world. There is no financial reward being part of their world; only bad things could come out of this.

CHAPTER 45

In the late '70s and early '80s, medical students at Bellevue were white Anglo-Saxon Protestants.

There were a lot of factors that went into creating this disparity. Economics of course was the number one factor dictating this disparity. Young white males who have rich parents have an upper hand. Institutionalized racism also played a role. So the government decided to level the playing field. During this time they introduced affirmative action. This document would fix old ills of discrimination. The reality is that what they did was lower the standards so that African Americans and Latinos could get an education in fields such as law, engineering, and medicine, which for hundreds of years were the sole domain of the white Anglo-Saxon Protestant student. Not because African Americans or Latinos didn't have the mental acumen but because they didn't learn or have the support system required to compete in these fields. In these endeavors, a good foundation or education is required. It didn't matter that some of the individuals didn't have the qualifications major schools had to have a certain percentage of individuals of color be admitted into their programs. Affirmative action was a revolutionary idea that angered many whites. Here you had numerous individuals with superior credentials being passed over so an African American or Latino could be given a shot at the American dream. NYU, a medical teaching hospital that works in cahoots with Bellevue Hospital, had to acquiesce to these governmental demands.

Initially the beneficiaries of this revolutionary idea were Asians, mainly Chinese and Indians from India, but soon you began to see people of color. Women were waiting nearby getting ready to get in the game. They were also discriminated against, and they exploded on the scene. They now dominate the medical profession. Good for them.

You now had the melting pot of races and nationalities the government envisioned. The first Latino person I saw walking in a group of medical students at Bellevue Hospital was Roberto Gonzalez. I was proud of his accomplishments, and I went right up to him and thanked him. He opened the doors for everyone else.

Roberto Gonzalez was a stepping-stone, a guy who sacrificed everything to accomplish his goal. I'm not sure if without affirmative action, the lowering of these standards, he would have accomplished these goals. It is time to eliminate governmental intrusions and allow all students to achieve their goals on their own without big brother's favoritism. We don't want a free lunch. We want to compete and let them know that we are individuals with a gifted background. I am part of a race that built pyramids and contemplated the concept of zero many eons ago. Racism shouldn't be playing a part in my development. I was asked to be a motivational speaker by a bunch of idiots. The detox department at Bellevue thought it would be a good idea for me to help these individuals. I didn't know what I was doing. They needed a body to fill in. Why would they think I could help? This is the type of leadership they bring to the table. Most of the people in leadership don't have proper credentials to run anything. Nepotism, nepotism, nepotism. We have a new mafia at Bellevue. The Carribean mafia. From top to bottom, these people are corrupt, looking to get their hands on the money.

At Bellevue I was now being floated more often than not to the detox unit. I became an expert motivational speaker, and the staff liked that I had a good control over this population. They were the same guys I would run into at Rikers. This detox program is the worst possible program in Bellevue Hospital. It costs $1,500 to house an individual at this program for one day. The benefits are minuscule. This is a total abuse of resources. This medically supervised detox unit is often used by patients as a hotel. They come in to shit, shower, shave, and prepare themselves for the next drug and alcohol run. All this administration is concerned about is the Medicaid benefit card that eventually pays for this treatment. One guy spent 254 days in one year visiting these facilities. But all you hear from the doctors, nurses and counselors is how this unit is the highest revenue producing area at Bellevue. There's this misconception that a three-, four-, or five-day stay followed up by a 28 day rehab is going to solve their problems; it is crazy.

Working with these patients made me feel somewhat like a hypocrite since I was struggling myself with cocaine, alcohol, and cigarettes. But since I was coming to work every day, I would justify my actions by saying I was a functioning addict. That's a misnomer. If you're drugging and drinking, you are not functioning. These were my personal demons clouding my judgment. My defense was down. I was beginning to make lots of mistakes. I got busted for drinking and driving, something I would never do in the past.

It would be easier for the medical profession to cure your rheumatoid arthritis, diabetes, heart disease than to cure the disease of addiction. This is what most of these professionals don't understand. They are just throwing their money away. The only reason why they continue to use 20 South for detox is the money, which involves millions a year.

We don't help these individuals. There are too many variables involved to be able to cure this disease.

Most of the individuals that come to Bellevue seeking treatment for addiction have a multitude of problems that must be addressed before you can cure these social ills. 60 to 75 percent of these individuals are homeless, which is a major trigger. If I have to ride the F train and use it as my blanket, my bed, and my pillow, I want to be fucked up, I don't want people to come in to the subway and see me lying there at two o'clock in the morning. They also have lost family contact, lost jobs, been incarcerated—all triggers. But this unit makes a lot of sense for Bellevue financially, and as long as there's a Bellevue Hospital, they will have a system in place like this because of the money.

But when you're an addict, you refuse to accept your deficiencies, anything to justify your behavior, and that's what I was doing, trying to rationalize my problem.

When you're in the grips of this disease, everyone around you suffers. In a matter of a few years, I lost my father, mother, brother, and sister. That was a good enough excuse for me to continue driving and drinking. I was the only one standing, and that hurt. So what better way to kill the pain than to constantly blow your mind with drugs and alcohol?

CHAPTER 46

I found myself in South Beach, Miami, the narcotic capital of the world at the time. The Colombians began transporting huge amounts of cocaine through the Florida Keys. Cuban nationals who had arrived from Mariel wanted to muscle the Columbian drug business. Take control of the narcotic trade in South Beach, Miami, Florida. A narcotic war exploded all over Florida. The effects of this conflict affected the whole East Coast of the United States to the heart of New York City, where the price of a kilo of cocaine doubled to $20,000.

I had a patient who was a mule asked by a New York City crime organization to pick up five kilos of cocaine in South Florida. He was given a $10,000 commission for the job. A few weeks later he was asked to pick up another five kilos. Angel Flores was now running back and forth from New York City to Florida picking up large amounts of cocaine. One day he decided to buy a house in the outskirts of Fort Lauderdale. Property at that time was cheap. He put down $5,000 and became a homeowner. The next time he went down to pick up cocaine for this New York City crime organization, he put another $5,000 down on a property near Miami. Angel began to buy his own supply, and it became very lucrative for him, transporting nearly a ton of cocaine within the next decade.

For over twelve years Angel continued to purchase properties all over the East Coast corridor between Florida and New York. He had properties in North and South Carolina, Georgia, Pennsylvania, Delaware, New Jersey, anywhere he could plop down $5,000 and get a mortgage. Angel had accumulated over 350 properties with a rental income of well over $300,000 a month. You try to be inconspicuous, but when you own that amount of property, you stand out like a sore thumb. The feds had an ongoing investigation about his dealings. Angel had decided to get out of the business. He was living comfortably with great wealth.

A few months had passed by when a local came to him and asked to purchase four kilos. Angel brushed him off, claiming he was not in that type of business. But this young guy was persistent. He continue to pester Angel about selling him four kilos. But Angel wouldn't budge. He told him flat out to leave him alone. This local yokel came back a few months later and continued to ask Angel to provide him with a connection. Angel really had not gotten the business out of his blood. And the temptation to make another run was still on his mind. He had a fascination about making money that wouldn't go away. It was an insatiable addiction for him. Finally, after over a year of relentless harassment by the local yokel, Angel decided to make another run.

When Angel got back to New York City he was fully loaded with a large stash. For Angel the attraction of money was overwhelming, he loved it. After dropping off the local yokel's four kilos, he drove to New Jersey to unload the rest. By the time he got back to his house a load of undercover cops in unmarked cars had staked out his place. After being found guilty at trial the Feds confiscated all of his properties including $25 million in cash. Angel should have gone with his instincts and he would have remained outside the arms of the law.

Two empty bottles of Bacardi were found in my office. I was taken to labor relations. My problem was escalating to where I had lost control of my mental faculties. That's what happens when you do drugs and drink. Then I just remember walking out of the bar at three thirty in the morning unable to find my car. I spent two hours walking up and down city blocks, not being able to find it. During this time I was drinking sixteen-ounce cans of beer. When I finally located my car, I drove off. I was drunk out of my mind. That's the kind of attitude you develop, "I don't give a fuck."

I was on the highway going sixty miles an hour when I fell asleep. If it wasn't for the grooves on the side of the road that woke me up, I was a split second away from rear-ending the car in front of me. I could have killed myself that night or, worse, kill someone else. The trouble with the addict is that he doesn't learn from his mistakes. That should've been a wake-up call, but I just thought of it as being lucky. Over the years I've had numerous close calls like that night. I was carrying three and a half grams of cocaine, an eight ball of cocaine for delivery when I got pulled over and busted for drunk driving. There was only one thing I could do—swallow it before the cops came to my car window. I spent two days locked up without taking a shit. I had no choice, or else I could have gotten busted for something worse, possession of a controlled substance. Again I brushed it off as being lucky. If any of those packages would have ruptured, I would've been in more trouble, and I knew that eventually my luck would run out.

I was desperate to get out of this business. I'd had enough. The problem here was that I was addicted to money and the good life it brought me. I thought of bringing in a partner to help me distribute the cocaine. The problem is you can't trust anybody. There are always leeches waiting to suck the blood out of you. But I knew the drug trade was coming to an end for me. I was somewhat egotistical in my thinking that I could become a big-time distributor. The thing is that once you cross that line, they won't let you get out of the game. Once you get to know the big-time players, you're in it for life. I couldn't risk being controlled that way. You make one mistake and you're done.

They also had strict rules. You couldn't be a user. You had to be a family man working. It was part of their disguise. You took care of business at night under the cover of darkness. The Colombians are people you don't want to fuck with unless you're suicidal.

At Rikers Island I had a few of these men facing humongous time for drug trafficking, life in prison. Not one of these men is willing to talk about a case for fear that they may be labeled a snitch. All the feds want is to snag a kingpin. If one of these men would talk, their sentence would be drastically reduced, perhaps even dismissed. But there's a large price to pay for such indiscretion on their part. Rat them out and you will get your throat cut from ear to ear and your family will disappear. Those are the choices: spend the rest your life behind bars in prison or get assassinated along with your family. If it were me, I think I would make a deal as long as my family is in the witness protection program. I would sing like a canary. But this is just fantasy. I wouldn't want to put my family in such a precarious situation. That's why trying to be a major distributor of narcotics was out of the question for me. I had a good run, it was time to get out of the game before any major injury occurred.

Then there is the heroin business, which is largely the domain of the Asians. Look around at Rikers Island and you see a handful of Asians incarcerated. Mostly for killing their families. Never for the trafficking of heroin. I can recall the last arrest of an individual for trafficking of heroin happened about twenty-two years ago. He was busted at the Waldorf Astoria with forty kilos of heroin. The best heroin in the world comes from the jungles of South Asia, known as the golden triangle. But nobody talks about this pipeline of heroin flooding the US market.

This supercrop is often overlooked and overshadowed by the warmongering activities going on in the Middle East. Today the bad guys come from this region of the world, and Afghanistan gets the blame for our addiction to heroin. The Asians are very smart people. They don't get involved in the street-level distribution of narcotics. They sell you the brick, kilos of heroin, tons of it, and have a virtual monopoly on this product. Yet look around Rikers Island and you don't find one Asian who has been arrested for the sale of heroin. Their banking system launders billions of dollars every year, the whole system that they run is different from ours.

A few of these young clinicians had the gall to fall in love with these degenerates. Another clinician, this guy was a supervisor no less, thought that bringing alcohol and cigarettes would make him popular. He was arrested at his house, which he was still paying the mortgage on, handcuffed, and brought to Nassau County Jail. The list of fools is endless.

You don't become a forensic clinician at one of the most violent jails in all of New York overnight. It takes years and a desire on your part to be the best. My first day on the job, I was told by a correction officer who was drunk out of his mind that you never make deals with the guys. Back then virtually all corrections officers drank. It was an acceptable culture. But I never forgot his advice to this day. I still don't make deals with anybody who is locked up or connected with the mob. Joanne who is a feisty Italian stallion, who bragged about being connected with the mob, ran into my office at Rikers Island and whispered, "Have you heard the latest?"

She stood about five feet one, but she had the heart of a lioness.

"What happened this time?" I asked.

"Bobby got busted bringing in K2 and marijuana in a lubricant jar," she whispered again.

"Bobby who?" I inquired.

"You know him, the Filipino social worker," she said.

"I knew him as Cruz. That's his first name, Bobby?" I asked.

"Yeah, Bobby Cruz," she continued to whisper, trying not to bring attention to herself. "According to some reports, blood gang members threatened to hurt his kids if he didn't cooperate," she stated.

"I thought he had an alternative lifestyle, wasn't he gay?" I asked.

"Bobby fathered two kids before he accepted the fact that he was gay," she told me.

Four captains walked into S mod, where our offices were located, and escorted him down to intake, where IG (intelligence gathering) arrested him on multiple felony charges.

It seemed surreal that another clinician thought that he could get over and be successful at bringing contraband into the facility. The temptation could overwhelm anyone. A pack of cigarettes would easily generate $1,000. This is why corrections officers are paid large sums of money to avoid corruption.

Joanne was not done. She kept rambling on about the problems with corrections. "Give me a fuckin break," she was angry that Bobby had been arrested.

"Listen," I told her, "he fucked up. Let it go."

She was aware that not long ago her intimate friend Vicky had been arrested for bringing glasses into the Rikers Island facility.

Joanne was still a neophyte when it came to dealing with this population, trying to understand the complexities that was Rikers Island. It takes a long time to get a grasp of what goes on at these facilities. You're dealing with the criminally insane, not your typical population.

A bag of Top or Bugler loose tobacco costs $3.35 at any cigarette shop. I can't tell you how many times since cigarettes were outlawed at the Rock that I've been offered $100 for a bag of loose tobacco. They charge $10 for a toothpick-size cigarette. They could make about 45 to 55 of these cigarettes from one bag of tops. So you have to figure that the temptation for these young clinicians to make a quick buck is overwhelming. The signs are posted all over the facility about bringing in contraband, and you could be facing a seven-year sentence.

CHAPTER 47

I was floated to Rose M. Singer, one of the worst experience in my career. This is the women's house of detention, filled with the most devious, degenerate girls in the five boroughs of New York City. Women who were sexually, physically, and emotionally abused since early childhood. Nearly 100 percent of these ladies are single moms with substance-abuse problems. This is a growing population that will explode in the coming years due in large part to lack of support systems. They are sexually promiscuous, looking for a knight in shining armor.

Many suffer from depression, have had children with multiple partners, and have poor coping skills. Their main asset is a pussy, which they pass around like candy to get what they want. Mainly drugs. I was able to see the pain in their eyes when I first began working with them. But they were wild and out of control. At first they tried to read me to see where I was coming from, if I could be one of their victims, or which way they could use me. I still had a personal ethical code to guide me. I would not step beyond these boundaries. I was raised by five women who taught me to respect the opposite sex and revere motherhood.

I was ill equipped to handle what came next. A cavalcade of piranhas trying to rape me. I was in shock, perturbed, unable to understand this twisted logic. Why would these low-life women think I feel comfortable in this situation that they have total control over?

One of these women came running down the hallway and sat down next to me and began to masturbate. She told me "she would like to be on an island with just men." It didn't matter to her if they were black, Latino, Chinese, or green, just as long as they were men. "And you're so cute," she told me. "I would put you at the head of the line."

I told her, "Thank you."

She continued to masturbate in front of me. She asked me if I was Italian. I told her I was Puerto Rican She got so excited and said, "You're Puerto Rican!!!"

I told her, "Please go masturbate yourself somewhere else."

She said, "I'm not jerking off, I am pleasuring myself."

I had numerous problems with this population. They lacked boundaries and self-respect and had no dignity. Sex was the common denominator in their lives. One woman brushed her pussy hair right in front of me and asked, "Do you like what it looks like, I'll give you some. My next door neighbor tells me it smells like roses?" Did she think I was impressed by this behavior?

Rose M. Singer was becoming a nightmare for me. They were showing me their tits and ass like it was something joyful. They were just crazy girls trying to get an upper hand, and they thought I would fall for their antics. But that's life in Rikers Island. Everything is a *tricky tricky*. There's always a solution to a problem. It's just that most people don't know how to get there.

I explained to the administration the horror stories and I would appreciate it if I was not floated back to Rose M. Singer. They granted my wish.I am a made man at Rikers Island, but that doesn't mean I can't get shot. I am an honorary gang member by default. Throughout my career I've given my patients the utmost respect, and that is why I'm able to enter into this most hostile environment on the planet and feel safe. I'm protected, respected, and given free rein to work my magic. They know I'm there to uplift their spirits, not to judge their actions. It's strange to feel comfortable with forty-seven men who have mental illness and personal issues who can be explosive at times. The anger they have can be seen everywhere around me, but I seem to defuse it whenever I enter into one of these units.

One day before cameras were deployed throughout Rikers Island, I walked into mod 11 B unit hungover and smelling like booze. A client noticed I needed help and told me to sit down in front of the TV. Twenty to twenty-five of the clients surrounded me, and I heard Mr. Robinson say, "Go to sleep."

It felt surreal to be comforted by these murderers, rapists, child molesters, and common thieves. But there I was snoring away while my clients pretended to be watching TV. I spent nearly two hours oblivious to the world around me. I finally woke up out of my stupor and thanked the guys for helping me out.

"Mr. Robinson, may I have a few minutes of your time?" I asked this murderous blood gang leader who always showed me respect. I told him, "Thanks for looking out."

"Don't worry, Doctor Rubildo," he said. "I got your back."

I said, "I'm not a doctor."

"You're a doctor to us," he proclaimed with a smile across his fat face, and then he winked at me.

I was still in a fog when I left the unit. I called central control for an emergency annual leave and left the premises. It felt good to think my clients would stick up for me to the very end. For me, it's a privilege to be servicing this odd clientele because I get it. They'll put their lives on the line if you treat them with respect. This is what the corrections department fails to understand when it comes to having control.

There is an unwritten manual provided to every individual on earth that will help you navigate any social setting. It's called respect.

I have different modalities that I use to pacify them, and they look forward to me getting there. Chess is a mainstay in the jail and prison system. You can place this game on top of a table and no one will break it. I've seen telephones, TVs, and radios smashed to pieces, but I've yet to see a chess set be defaced by an inmate. It's just an odd occurrence, the respect shown for this game. It's given an angelic quality. I've played this game since I was seven years old. I played well over three hundred thousand games. When I walked into one of these units, I'm immediately challenged by someone who wants to dethrone me. They line up to take their turn.

Dominoes have the same kind of adoration. No one will disturb a set of dominoes sitting on the table. My grandfather taught me how to play, so I also have a long history in this game. The beauty of both of these games is that they are mathematical equations that keep your mind alert at all times. They have a medicinal property and are helpful in maintaining you healthy.

It took me a lot of energy to get where I am today. I spent a googolplex of hours trying to master my trade. Although I feel I have accomplished a certain amount of success, there's still room for improvement. No one could ever know everything about a certain subject matter, especially with this population. It's an ever-changing landscape that baffles you. When you think you've heard everything, something else comes along that shocks you with fear. Recently there was a guy housed at Rikers who went on a killing rampage. He assassinated both of his parents. After leaving his parents in a pool of blood, he left the house and killed a few more people along the way, randomly shooting them for no apparent reason. He then entered a subway station with intent to commit suicide.

He jumped headfirst into the train. His face was mangled beyond recognition, but he survived. He needed over 300 stitches to reconstruct the face. He is a paranoid schizophrenic who stopped taking his medication. This is a debilitating disease. The only way to control it is through chemical intervention or a lobotomy. Back in the 1920s and 1930s, the way Bellevue treated a mentally challenged patient with psychotic features was to hose you down with cold water. That was the remedy back then. Bellevue later became instrumental in the development of the initial miracle psych medications such as Haldol and Thorazine.

Clarity of thought is impossible to measure. It has been suggested that the Puritan values of hard work is what created the wealth of this country, and the ideology of our forefathers gave it its greatness.

The great genius Thomas Jefferson stated that there should be a revolution every twenty years to get rid of corruption. Why would a figure of this magnitude promote an overthrow of a government he engineered to establish? This is the beauty of his insight that he could project or see the corruption of unchecked power. This was a unique person who had the foresight to envision the evils of corruption. He was able to foresee that that institutions like Bellevue and later Rikers Island could have an inherent corrupt culture due to human frailties.

CHAPTER 48

I was twenty-three years old hanging out in salsa and disco clubs, trying to connect with a super lifestyle. I wanted to be rich and enjoy the good things that come with being financially independent. I had my own business at this time, construction. I thought I was on top of the world. When I got home I always had extensive energy for work. After working at the group home from five to ten, my buddy Rob and I would run to the clubs and hang out till three in the morning.

It mattered little to me that I had a beautiful girl at home raising my family. I had my own agenda. It seemed like I had a death wish trying to destroy the most beautiful thing I had, my family. I know she didn't sign up for this, but I didn't give a fuck. I was selfish, self-centered, and egotistical. I just wanted to party and have a good time. She made me feel tied down, and I didn't like it, not at all. But that's what happens when you're twenty-four, twenty-five, or twenty-six years old and drugging and drinking. You have a tendency to make big mistakes. I didn't feel like I was married. It took me a long time to realize what I had. She would take a bullet for me.

It was in the bathroom of one of these clubs that I had my first taste of cocaine. I found out one thing that night; I loved cocaine. I was already fucked up on alcohol and marijuana when someone gave me a line for each nostril. Soon after taking these two lines, my brain froze. I had no idea where I was or what I was doing. That was the whole idea, to forget all my problems. For well over an hour I was in paradise. Nothing bothered me that night. Soon after I came back down, the problems were still there. My escape from reality was temporary.

That night, or should I say morning, my baby's mama was furious. She wanted to kill me. You could see it in her eyes. I reeked of alcohol, marijuana, and cigarettes, and my nose was encrusted in powder cocaine. The poison was oozing out of my pores. I was the poster child for addiction.

It's a good thing that my cocaine connection at the time died in a horrific car accident. His head was decapitated while going ninety miles an hour. I'm not sure I would've survived this ordeal if he hadn't died. After his death, things went back to being normal, going to work and coming straight home. I got tired of hanging out. I even stopped smoking marijuana and for good reason. My old lady called me at work and asked if I could pick up a box of Pampers. I only had $5 to my name, and they cost $1.19. Today that same box costs over $40. I decided to ask my marijuana dealer for credit. He told me he didn't give out credit to anybody. I said "I've been picking up my marijuana from you for the last eight months, you can't give me a little credit? You can come here for eight years and I still won't give you credit," he said to me.

When I got down to the sidewalk, I had to make a decision whether to buy the Pampers or buy my $5 bag of marijuana. My son won out. I didn't like the fact that this individual had such control over me. I never picked up another joint again.

CHAPTER 49

I am always asked by my friends how it feels to work at Bellevue prison ward for the criminally insane and Rikers Island mental observation area. It's difficult for the average layperson to understand the dynamics involved in working with this population or in these areas. It's like trying to explain quantum physics to a five-year-old.

They are captivated by the stories I tell them, amused! But they can't capture the vivid reality that's produced on a daily basis by these violent domains.

There are so many factors and variables that come into play with this population, it's impossible to detail exactly what goes on here. Bellevue and Rikers Island are the most fascinating places I've ever worked in. They are constantly changing, and in the process I get further educated. You can't go to a book and get this type of education. You have to experience it. Even individuals who have gone through this experience can't give proper credence. They are just intriguing places to work in.

The corruption that is innate to both of these large institutions can sometimes have an numbing quality.

I wish I could wave a magic wand and enlighten everyone around me about these conditions, the trouble that permeates throughout these institutions and the corruption that would not go away.

Some of these guys I've known for the past forty years. They've been in and out of the joint. After a while they get acclimated to being locked up. They can't survive living outside of jail or prison. Life behind bars has a tendency to preserve you. No telephone bill, no electric bill, there's nothing to worry about except doing your time, and after a while you learn to cope with that. They are provided with the best medical plan in New York State. Therefore, the stress level is greatly reduced. The food, which smells like crap, is healthy.

There was a guy who every October would throw a brick through a restaurant window simply so he could be incarcerated between October and May. It was his way to avoid the winter months. He preferred to be locked up during this time than to be walking the streets of New York City freezing. This is the warped mentality we medical professionals have to deal with on a daily basis. It's the big fish in a small pond versus the little fish in the big pond. Most of these individuals, once they leave incarceration, are unable to cope in the outside world, so they'd rather be locked up because they have control there.

Brad H. was a patient at C 71, the mental observation unit at Rikers Island. He had been arrested fifty-five times. He brought a lawsuit against the city of New York. He claimed there was not enough support systems for individuals once discharged from Rikers Island; therefore, it was a revolving door for him when he got out. He stated that he was being set up for failure. So to remedy this situation, the city of New York spent millions with minimal results. There are hundreds of individuals who fall under this category. Many are homeless, jobless, and with little prospects. Nearly all of them end up in New York City shelters, which is the worst place to be if you're in addict. Since 75 to 85 percent of incarcerated individuals have a substance-abuse problem, the odds of them making it out in the streets are slim to none.

Many of these guys have no shot at being productive citizens of society. They have bounced back and forth from Rikers Island to the street and to the mental hospitals for so long that this has become their job. The reality is that no amount of money allocated by the city of New York will cure this problem. This type of behavioral dynamics is ingrained into these individuals' psyche, patterns that have developed over a long period of time that require intensive therapeutic interventions. Only if you're willing to bankrupt the city of New York and it still wouldn't help.

Before you could say presto, chango, alakazam, one of our newly minted clinicians got busted for bringing in contraband. When something like this happens that your all-American girl has to be escorted off the premises, all kinds of rumors abound. First she was having an inappropriate affair with one of the inmates. Then it was said that she brought in a pair of reading glasses for one of her patients. So you don't know what to believe. Unfortunately for this young lady, she was doing all of the above and more. She didn't only bring in a pair of glasses; she brought in seven pairs. It was not one individual that she was flirting with; it was numerous. What is it about these young girls that fall in love with such degenerates, what is the motivating factor? We now hear that she has been visiting an inmate in upstate New York. I'm told it's possible that the IG, the investigative department, in Rikers Island is planning to arrest her. These are serious charges.

Whose fault is this? Perhaps the administration didn't do enough to avoid these pitfalls with a relatively new, green-around-the-edges clinician who is just starting out her career. These are cunning cons who are experts at manipulation. Once you make a mistake and acquiesce to their underhanded suggestions, your job is dead. You might as well start packing your office trinkets and saying good-bye to coworkers and at the same time start looking for a new job. Frontline staff such as Mr. Brown, Mr. Blatt, and myself are often overlooked in training these new recruits, who are never in touch with this population. The extent of Administration's contact is walk-throughs. Instead, this task is given to others. They basically sit in white ivory towers spewing commands from afar. This is why large bureaucracies such as Bellevue and Rikers Island have such difficulty operating in the black. There's always an extra added cost inherent in their overall operation.

In late October, Bellevue contracted out the installation of an elaborate menagerie of Christmas decorations to be placed all around the hospital. The cost runs into hundreds of thousands of dollars. Every year it happens like clockwork. Whose great idea was this, and what sort of kickback is that individual getting? The vast reservoir of cash at Bellevue's disposal is mind-boggling. Why is it that I'm not allowed to tap into this enormous wealth? If I were given the opportunity to handle such funds, there would be no reason for me to sell drugs. In fact, more than half of the individuals in close proximity to the cash don't even have credentials to be working in these areas.

Bellevue's soul has been so tarnished and battered over the past decades by these decrepit administrators it's difficult for me to even contemplate stealing a toothbrush.

I hate thieves. There's just something about them that makes me feel uneasy. They're sneaky, underhanded, and can't be trusted. In Rikers there are hundreds of these characters awaiting trial. It's funny how people play with words. Someone breaks into a car and steals a couple of dollars from the glove compartment; it's called petty theft. On the other hand, a person like Luis Velez embezzles $600,000 from a Cola company, and they call that a white-collar crime. It doesn't matter whether you're stealing $6 or $600,000. You're still a thief. But by far the most astute thief on the planet is your heroin addict. These individuals wake up with zero dollars and within two or three hours have $200 in their pockets. It's a special gift, an art form they have developed over the years to survive. This ability is uncanny.

CHAPTER 50

According to detectives, a young prostitute had been murdered and her body dumped in Flushing Meadows Park overnight.

Debbie Thomas, who made her living walking around Roosevelt Avenue, was well known by the local street urchins who frequented the area. She had given more blowjobs than the FBI has fingerprints on file. That was her specialty. She was also a psych patient at Bellevue Hospital, 20 East MICA (mental illness chemical abuse unit). She had been treated by Dr. Burton for many years. Dr. Burton drove around in a super-juiced-up van you could practically live in. We later found out from the medical examiner's office that Debbie had a heart attack brought on by high levels of cocaine use. But since the body had been moved, it was ruled a homicide. According to detectives, a young prostitute had been murdered and her body was dumped in Flushing Meadows Park overnight.

On numerous occasions I had seen Dr. Burton drive by the area. I used to ask myself, why would Dr. Burton be around here? Apparently he was one of her customers. Months later Dr. Burton was picked up and charged with criminally negligent homicide. They had been together inside the van smoking crack cocaine when she keeled over and died. His best thinking that night was to drive inside Flushing Meadows Park and dump the body into the bushes. The best lawyers in the world were unable to get him off this hook.

Ethically, Dr. Burton was corrupt. That, more than anything else, was his downfall. You just don't go around getting blowjobs from your patients while smoking crack cocaine with them. Dr. Burton was handed down a fifteen-year sentence. He later committed suicide.

The reason why Dr. Burton was prosecuted is the terminology known as the line of causation. Things that were placed in motion by Dr. Burton had a direct effect on her death. Dr. Burton's ethical and moral bankruptcy was viewed by the court as contrary to the scope of his medical training. Law is a philosophy that encompasses the whole human experience and can ignite massive debates concerning ethics. What would the common man do under similar situations?

In another scenario, a patient who had been brought to Bellevue Hospital prison ward for the criminally insane on a suicide watch told me that Dr. Taylor" who had just walked into the treatment room where I was interviewing said patient "owes me $20." I asked him why? "I gave him a blowjob and he never paid me." He also told me that he had been his patient on 18 North, you can't make this up.

When I first came to Bellevue, sexual activity was out of control. Half of the workforce had an alternative lifestyle. In the beginning of the 1980s, if you walked around the medical areas of our great facility, you would see employees lying in bed sick. They didn't know what it was then, but HIV wiped out one-third of our employees. The era of free love was over, and the bill was due. The losses were staggering. Liberace, Rock Hudson, fashion designers, painters, poets were all affected by this debilitating, deadly disease. Magic Johnson who contracted HIV from a famous prostitute, had to retire from the NBA.

The artistic drainage caused by HIV is still being felt to this day. What genius was lost to this epidemic cannot be measured. Was there a Michael Angelo or Leonardo da Vinci among the dead? Someone once told me that the universe was created by a race a superaliens. What mind can contemplate this idea? The notion that a great mind was lost to the ravages of AIDS saddens me.

CHAPTER 51

I was offered an opportunity to run guns from South Carolina by a childhood friend whose full-time job was to rob banks. I ran into Henry on Smith Street and Butler in Brooklyn near my linoleum and carpet store, which I later turned into a construction company. Henry was always dressed like a Wall Street businessman, with alligator shoes, three-piece suit, and a gift for gab. Under his suit jacket he carried a sawed-off shotgun. Who would think that this guy was a crook? He was unassuming. You couldn't pick him out in a crowd. But he was an intellectual beating the odds. He insisted that we go into business together.

I had heard that gunrunning was profitable, but it had to be in large quantities. Two or three guns would not make you any money. I was impressed with Henry's cold demeanor. He had ice running through his veins. The plan was to bring fifty Glock nines in the first shipment at a price of $200. To make a profit, we had to sell them at $300. The selling point of this endeavor was that the guns were given to us on consignment with a certain amount of time allowed to be paid back in full. I knew by now that this was a dangerous undertaking. You better have the money when the time ran out, or else you could pay with your life. You don't want to fuck around with these hillbillies because they would shoot you from one hundred yards away.

I told Henry that I could probably get rid of five or ten guns at most through Bellevue. But to my surprise, everyone at Bellevue was looking to arm themselves. It was a classic case of supply and demand; my price went up. I didn't need to tell Henry that there was a huge demand for guns at Bellevue Hospital and I was planning to raise my price. Henry's domain was with the hood. He had lots of connections there. I'm sure he didn't tell me about his added cost to the pieces he was selling, so in return I added another hundred dollars to the hardware I sold.

Under the Bloomberg administration, tobacco almost became illegal. We were going down to South Carolina, the cigarette capital of the world.

Guns and cigarettes were the battle cry against Michael Bloomberg, that motherfucker who made billions of dollars and don't tell me he didn't do illegal shit in his life. In order to make quality cash, you had to bring dozens and dozens of guns into the city.

This nanny, overbearing mayor wants to abolish a constitutional amendment. Our forefathers didn't need instructions to create the most amazing document the free world has ever experienced. The right to bear arms is explicitly stated in this phenomenal legacy left to us by our forefathers. If we were able to eliminate this privilege of bearing arms thugs would still be able to purchase guns. We have laws that prohibit us from procuring narcotics, but people are still getting high. Prohibition restricted the sale of alcohol, but my great grandfather was still able to drink his moonshine.

The same guy who allegedly bought his way into another election and I blame black folks for not coming out simply because it was raining that day. This guy, Michael Bloomberg, spent about $100 million dollars to run for a third term, when two terms were the legal limit set by law.. We haven't heard the last of this fucking nanny, he is going to be involved with us for a long time, just another politician trying to tell us what to do. He was worth $7 billion when he came into office. At the end of his third term, he was worth $30 billion. So don't tell me that he got this money by being a Christian. How is this possible? Maybe we should give him another term to help him out?

CHAPTER 52

I had an uneasy feeling that I was being stalked by some of the workers at Bellevue. They knew I often carried large sums of money on my person; $3,000 to $4,000 after payday was not unusual for me to have on my person. I took as much precaution as I possibly could, parking my car in the south parking lot of the building and giving the attendant a couple of dollars so he could have my car ready to go as soon as my tour of duty was done. I also bought an equalizer, a seventeen-shot Glock nine, and I kept it loaded at all times. I would not hesitate to plug a couple of shots into somebody if I was going to be injured.

I knew the deal. Most of the support staff at Bellevue came from the hood. Nursing Assistants, transporters, housekeepers, they couldn't be trusted. I had run into some of them at Rikers Island.

It was bad enough that some of my patients when released from jail would hang out in front of Bellevue. Now I have to watch my back with a new tier of thugs who wanted to rip me off. I had to be cautious with the staff.

Years ago a lady who was selling jewelry like myself had her locker broken into, and $24,000 in cash and about $50,000 worth of jewelry were stolen. You could hear her screams down the hallway when she found out everything was gone. She cried for over two weeks. These are activities that can't be reported to the police, so she had to just swallow the loss.

She was partly to blame for bragging about all the things she had all the time. I always wanted to keep a low profile, didn't want anybody to know what I was doing.

The $24,000 she had on hand was to cash staff members' paychecks, which was part of her business. There was no direct deposit. If you wanted to cash your check, you would go to the check-cashing place and pay about $6. She gave them a discount at $3. She had about eighty customers and was making a pretty penny back in the early 1980s.

She had been targeted for a long time. They are constantly looking for your weaknesses, and when the opportunity presents itself, they jump on it. No one is immune from these predators. That's why I was always looking over my shoulder. I never let them catch me off guard. You develop a sixth sense to these dangers.

I always kept my hand wrapped around the equalizer, a sort of preventive medicine. I wasn't going to get caught out there naked.

To a certain degree I was being a little grandiose, but my mind kept thinking about these possibilities and how I would handle them. Don't get me wrong, I was prepared to kill somebody if their intention was to hurt me. I had no doubt in my mind this is the way I would react.

I had gone down to Water Street to deliver a package of cocaine. The projects down there were dangerous. It was late at night, and I knew I had to go in and out as quickly as possible. Make one mistake down there and you could be in big trouble. My customer asked me to stay a while. I told her no, that I got to go. But she insisted. I told her I would stay for a few minutes. A few minutes turned into a couple of hours. It was about twelve o'clock when I left. I decided to walk down the stairs so I could exit through the rear of the building and save a few steps. It was a pitch-black winter night. Soon after

I started walking the corridor between the buildings, three to four adolescent males began to follow me. I knew I had made a mistake. I heard them say, "We could scramble some brains tonight." I already had my hand on my gun. They kept mocking me, referring to the fact that they were going to splatter my brain onto the sidewalk. I had on a long leather trench coat to hide my piece. I decided to lower my head to avoid getting hit. I wasn't sure if they carried weapons, but I was ready. About forty-five yards away, there was a lamppost shedding light on the sidewalk. I didn't panic. I continued to walk toward the lamppost. Their chatter was unabated, but as soon as I got close to the lamppost, they disappeared into the night. I felt a sense of relief. I never went back to that area unless it was daytime.

CHAPTER 53

Before the proliferation of cameras at Rikers Island and Bellevue Hospital prison ward, violence took place on a large scale. There were incidents with blood splattered on the ceiling, the walls, and all over the floor. It was a culture that everyone accepted as the norm. I personally witnessed people getting hit over the head with old-type radios that weigh three pounds. One guy was beaten to a pulp by corrections in the intake area. These were nasty guys back then, and anyone that stepped out of line would be dealt with immediately. They were judge, jury, and executioner all at the same time. They saw the medical staff as just another set of prisoners interfering in their domain. They failed to see the big picture. There were major changes coming, and the old dinosaurs were about to go extinct. 40 percent of the incarcerated population at Rikers Island has been identified as having mental illness. Treatment had to be altered to accommodate this growing reality.

Fifteen years ago there were no computers. We had to do all charting manually, writing it down. Staff consisted of just a few clinicians, myself, Bob Brown, Tony Blatt, Dr. Myers, and two administrators. We were trying to service over 450 mentally ill patients.

You hope no one committed suicide or you would be made the scapegoat.

Overnight three dozen clinicians popped out of nowhere, and C 71, the largest mental observation unit at Rikers Island, considered to be the highest form of mental health care inside C 95, was flooded with health-care providers. This was the new mantra, provide mental health care to a population that was in need of a new approach.

Treatment of the jail population has become very complicated. Corrections felt uncomfortable with this new approach of catering to criminals. A paramilitary outfit such as corrections always has a need to be in total control.

CHAPTER 54

Back when Henry and I began bringing guns into the city, a carton of cigarettes cost $17. This would become a new source of income. I could easily sell a carton for $50. I started small, twenty cartons at a time. There was a huge market for cigarettes. Cigarettes kept going up in price. They went from $6 a pack to $11, and the price pretty much remained the same at the wholesale level. Selling guns was one thing; selling cigarettes was something else. We received the guns on consignment. The cigarettes you had to have the money up front. You could easily be hijacked. It was very dangerous working with cigarettes. The police were always patrolling near the Indian reservation looking for people who bought large numbers of cigarettes. Then there were the locals always looking out to hijack somebody from out of state. New York State plates stood out like a sore thumb. We were easy targets.

If I could get rid of the whole shipment at once, I would give a better price, $40 a carton. On the other hand, if it was dribs and drabs, then it would be $50 a carton. This would be a direct cash transaction, no credit.

These were bad hombres I was dealing with. You couldn't take a chance and let down your guard. They would buy your cigarettes, turn around, and hold you up for the money.

If you're walking at two o'clock in the morning into the Marcy projects, between Myrtle and Flushing Avenue, in the heart of Brooklyn, with one hundred cartons of cigarettes, you better be carrying a piece. After making a few transactions, I got to know the crew. They would escort me from the courtyard up to the fifth floor. The kingpin I was working with seemed pretty honorable. I told him I had cocaine and guns. Immediately we formed a partnership. Hakeem had long black dreadlocks down past his buttocks, with an Olympic physique that made women drool. He was a handsome black man whose main contribution to this point had been flooding his neighborhood with the best Jamaican ganja. That's all he talked about when we first crossed paths while I was signing a client who had been injured in a subway accident.

He asked me, "Have you ever smoked in a chalice?"

I told him, "I have no idea what you're talking about."

He said, "It's a contraption made out of the calabaza plant with a long rubber hose attached at the bottom. You fill it up with marijuana and smoke all day, man." Hakeem was never too far away from a pound of the finest Jamaican ganja, always stoned out of his mind and listening to reggae.

"That's cool," I told him. "But I have a little proposition that may interest you."

Immediately he became focused on my every word. "Spill it, my man. What you got to say?" he asked.

"I'm in the wholesale business. I sell cocaine, guns, and cigarettes," I told him.

"I could use the guns and the cigarettes. But I don't want to fuck with that cocaine. I don't want my crew getting involved with that bullshit, it's too dangerous," he said.

"This is a package deal, my brother. You either take all three or we don't do business," I told him. "Besides," I continued to explain to him, "you already have the marijuana infrastructure in place. All you have to do is convert your runners into selling cocaine and you will quadruple your profits within a month."

He got up from his chair and began pacing around the room, trying to figure this thing out. "There's always collateral damage involved in these types of operations. So you lose one or two of your crew members. You have an endless supply of these young kids running around here, they can be easily replaced," I told him.

"You don't get it," he said in an angry tone of voice. "Some of these kids running in my crew are blood relatives. How am I going to face their mothers and tell them their son is now a cocaine junkie?" he said.

"Are you kidding me?" I asked. "My jail is full of junkies that started out smoking marijuana and graduated to hard narcotics," I told him. "You are selling marijuana, aren't you?" I asked. "So the seed has already been planted for their self-destruction to occur."

He sat back down, poured some marijuana into a pipe, and began to smoke. He extended his arm across the table and shook my hand. "We got a deal," he said.

I can now tell you the first time I was escorted to the fifth-floor apartment in this filthy project. I was scared. All these young African American males scared the shit out of me. Lucky for me, Hakeem was a shrewd businessman whose love for money could never be satisfied. Hakeem and his crew were busted as a drug enterprise. I believe he is still locked up. That's the biggest problem with this business; people disappear. One minute you are making millions and on top of the world; the next, you're behind bars facing twenty-five to life.

As I was being escorted to Hakeem's apartment, I looked around and saw these young African American males between the ages of fourteen and seventeen years of age playing gangsta. Walk into most city projects, and the same scenario is being played out across the five boroughs of New York. Adolescent black males working the drug and gun trade with masterful skills. And mothers pray that their eleven-, twelve-, or thirteen-year-old daughters won't grow breasts. These young bucks are relentless in their pursuit to fuck them, and the end result is a new generation of throwaway kids.

Hakeem's prophecy turned out to be true. Some of his young crew members began using their own supply and fell victim to the criminal justice system. I've run into some of them while out in Rikers Island, detoxing from powerful narcotics such as heroin, Percocets, Roxies, and Xanax. These behavioral dynamics are predicated on who does the nurturing during early childhood, and certainly Hakeem was not up to the task. I continue to bear witness to this horrific problem of one generation after another being locked up for drug use. What the politicians and police don't understand is that treatment and education will solve this problem, not incarceration.

There's an odd dichotomy in our social thinking when we are willing to subjugate innocent lives in the name of profit. The criminal justice system plays a role in this abuse. We allow alcohol to be consumed in this country by millions of metric tons. Catch an African American or Latino male with a couple of joints in their pocket and they throw them in jail for eight months. I can't start to quantify how many problems have been created by the consumption of alcohol in this country and around the world. It had been known since the 1920s that the prohibition of alcohol created an uncontrollable monster. The group of people who supported prohibition of alcohol quickly realized that it would not work. All it helped do was create millionaires out of gangsters. Today, street-level drugs and pharmaceutical opiate-based medication are creating a similar type of criminal element. We may have to start thinking the unconscionable of legalizing street-level narcotics and opiate-based pharmaceutical products. How else are we to rectify this inadequacy?

Ask a young black teenager what he would like to be when he grows up, and the first thing he would tell you is a rapper or a basketball player. Being a doctor, lawyer, or an engineer is the last thing on his mind. Yet it takes the same amount of hard work and effort to be either one. The only difference is that it takes a lot longer for a doctor, lawyer, or an engineer to generate a good income. While a professional basketball player and a rapper are showered with wealth immediately. So while Hakeem sits around in his apartment smoking ganja, making money, and fucking little girls, what other choice do these young men have since this is the guy they emulate? Their new-found father figure.

Education is always being tossed around as the great panacea to solving these social ills. It's not enough. The difficulty with this social disease is that it has so many tentacles, human variables, it is difficult to pinpoint the problem's origin.

Lack of a father figure, sexual molestation, substance abuse, dysfunctional parents, verbal and physical abuse, all can help ignite deviant behavioral patterns in early childhood.

When my children were growing up, they thought I was a god because I stood by them 100 percent at all times. They were able to depend on me to come through for them. I never shirk my respon-sibilities. My family was the most important thing in my life. Most of these young individuals helping Hakeem create wealth never even knew their fathers. You have to be a special person to recover from this type of trauma.

We are not reinventing the wheel here. Anthropologists and sociologists have been arguing about the merits of the nuclear family for centuries. In this country welfare has made it easy to abandon children by parents. Governmental interference is largely to blame for this explosion of throwaway kids.

CHAPTER 55

I never trusted men, whether selling drugs, making loans, or providing jewelry on consignment. They made me feel leery. I always had to look over my shoulder with them. Women always made me feel good. Guys were always trying to get over on me. This particular gentleman tried to get over on me, and I asked him to come to my office. I pulled my gun out and placed it on my desk. I told him I was running out of patience with him. I needed him to give me my money, or I would put a hole in his kneecap. He pulled out his wad of cash and placed $200 in my hand. Our business was done. This is the only type of language these individuals understood. There were others that needed to be addressed in a similar fashion. Aside from the cokehead doctors, I stopped doing business with guys they just weren't worth it. On the other hand women had the same mentality only thing that separates them from guys was that they had a pussy to barter. They were always ready to take down their panties for a couple of dollars. Gorgeous women were willing to give you a blowjob to reduce their debt. I often wondered whether they wanted to give me pussy because I was good-looking, or was it the money?

As far back as I can remember, I was always showered by women. It was easy for me to get laid. The best fuck I ever had in my life was by an older woman high on cocaine. I was nineteen years old and able to ejaculate three times within a half hour. She taught me how to slow down and satisfy a woman. Back then all I knew how to do was fuck and get my rocks off. I had no idea that fucking women was an art form. But here was this woman giving me lessons on how to fulfill her every need. I found out that women have a tremendous sexual endurance. She told me that it takes a real man to satisfy a woman sexually.

To this day I continue to follow her philosophical premise that women should be revered during sexual encounters. That's the one thing Bellevue women didn't understand. I wasn't going to throw my money away for a blowjob. It's not my style. But they continue to flirt with me and offer carnal knowledge. Don't get me wrong. I love pussy, but I love cash more. I wasn't in the habit of paying for pussy. It was always there for me, free. I'm very finicky when it comes to women, and if they are throwing themselves at you, they are not worth it. I like my women tall, thin, and with a brain. You can fuck just so much, and that gets stale quickly. I need a woman that is able to exchange ideas with me and carry an interesting conversation. The women I work with at Bellevue borrowed money from me were not the brightest lightbulbs. Many had personal issues. The Rikers Island women were a different animal altogether, loud, abusive, and just ugly personalities. It's difficult to find one woman in this crowd that has any class. Once you become part of corrections, your personality gets destroyed. You become void of feelings. You treat everyone like they're guilty, and you don't trust anybody.

At Rikers Island you didn't have the same type of freedom. I couldn't make loans or sell jewelry. I was unable to peddle drugs. I never tried. I knew that I was being closely monitored by these syco-phants. They had undercover cops watching my every move. They didn't trust me, and I was cool with that. If given the opportunity, I would run wild. There was a lot of money to be made behind the walls of Rikers. On numerous occasions I was offered $100 for a pack of cigarettes. They were not innovative; they offered the same $100 bill over and over and over again. They must've thought I was stupid, but I saw right through their scheme. After a while they stopped trying to set me up. I was not falling for their idiotic attempts at snagging me.

It took me a long time to learn how to run a motivational group, which eventually became my specialty. Most of my material came from the patients I worked with. The books I read were useless. They didn't really capture the essence of working with this population. I began to flourish as my experience increased. For years I had to write everything down and then regurgitate it back to the patients. Since I decided to stay longer at Bellevue than I expected, I decided I wanted to be the best possible therapist I could be.

If you look around today, corruption is in every segment of our city agencies.

When you are handling the amount of money I was making, you attract other elements besides your general lowlifes. The territory of Bellevue Hospital belonged to somebody, and they wanted to get paid. The five boroughs of New York City are carved up like a giant turkey by numerous ethnic groups. You can't operate without their protection. It all depends on who gets to you first, but you'll have to pay out to one of these groups. It just so happened that the crazy lady Irina, who wanted to run over her daughter-in-law with a car, had an idea of my personal business at Bellevue. That's why she approached me in the first place to murder her daughter-in-law. She thought I had some kind of connection to Murder Inc. That lunatic bitch talked to somebody about me and let the cat out of the bag. Everyone knew that the Russian mob was a crazy bunch that would kill you in a nanosecond if they didn't get their way. That dumb stupid bitch placed my life in jeopardy by opening her mouth.

I had to work late on Friday night at Bellevue. I went down to smoke a cigarette at around eight o'clock. On my way back, there were two guys standing near the elevator banks. When I walked into the elevator, they followed me. One of them turned to me and said in broken English with a Russian accent, "My boss wants to talk with you." I wasn't surprised. I knew this day was coming. It was just a matter of time. I just didn't think it would be the Russians who would make the first move. Once the word gets out that you're selling drugs, loan sharking, and ambulance chasing, someone is going to come knocking on your door. They would get back to me in a few days to set up a meeting.

That same night I went to meet up with my cocaine connection. I told him I didn't want Russians interfering with my business. He told me, "One way or another someone's going to get a piece of your pie. It all boils down to who you preferred to be making money off your back. They are all the same." He suggested I go with the Puerto Ricans. It's better to deal with your own kind. He gave me a cell phone and a name, Luis Serrano. I quickly arranged to have a meeting with Mr. Serrano, as he preferred to be called. I told him about my pending meeting with the Russkies. He told me from now on I would report to him and that he'd take care of the Russian. He said something like this could spark a war. He assured me that they wouldn't come after me. I was the moneymaker. They wanted to keep me alive. He reviewed my financial portfolio and said he would collect 15 percent on all of my businesses. The gold jewelry transactions I could keep for myself. The only way I could get out was to stop my business practice, and I would be charged a certain amount for getting out. He knew that everyone always underreported the amount of cash being made. As long as he didn't catch me, everything would be all right, but if he happened to find out about it, there would be consequences. He wanted his money twice a month, no excuses. So now I had a financial monkey on my back with the threat of physical violence if I didn't pay. My financial paradise, which I cultivated and nurtured for years, was now at the verge of collapse.

I never wanted a partnership, but I had no choice. It was either protection from the Puerto Ricans or the Russians. Either way, I was going to get fucked. I should run Irina over with a car. There were a few benefits that came out of this nonsense. I became a boss, and I had a loaded gun to use anytime I wanted. If someone failed to pay, I could send a couple of goons out to take care of them; that was my loaded gun.

There was a time when I was making $10,000 a week. At 15 percent that was $1,500 I was giving to this new monkey on my back. Of course I would never report that amount to Mr. Serrano. I'd rather take my chances and get my ass beaten than to give up my profits to this new motherfucker, Mr. Serrano. I couldn't believe what I'd gotten myself into with these individuals. Business was always a pleasure for me. It now became a chore. I felt trapped.

The staff at Bellevue Hospital has been conditioned to be corrupt. Personnel at Rikers Island work diligently to send the sickest individuals that need hospitalization to Bellevue. They require immediate chemical intervention in order to stabilize their psychotic symptoms. But the sycophants who run this great forensic institution are fearful of difficult patients. High-maintenance clients are not welcomed. They present a statistical nightmare for the bureaucracy that handles these high-profile individuals. We at Rikers sent numerous individuals who were a danger to self and others, but they refused to hospitalize them. They were more geared to handle malingerers. You can make a deal with them. Don't fuck up for the next few weeks and we'll let you hang out for a while. That's the way Bellevue Hospital operates today. You have to make deals with patients with antisocial personality disorder in order to keep stats within acceptable numbers.

Dr. Levine's only interest was to treat the patient's illness. He had been trained by Dr. Henry Sachs for over ten years on forensic medicine. He was sort of a father figure to him. Dr. Sachs was an old-school type who didn't take guff from any kind of patient. This kind of forensic medicine technique rubbed off on Dr. Levine. But like everyone else, Dr. Levine had demons he couldn't control. Women were his tragic flaw. If it wasn't because he was a doctor, he would've been arrested a long time ago for sexual harassment. Women tended to acquiesce to his flirtatiousness and give him a pass. Any female that would walk into his office was a prey. It was like a lamb stepping into a lion's den. He would molest them from head to toe with no consequences. He would spend thousands of dollars on telephone sex hotlines. But you couldn't question his psychiatric skills. He was outstanding at a genius level. He had a smooth demeanor able to flatter your ego with a few choice words. He wasn't an ivory-tower, white-picket-fence guy. He grew up in northern Manhattan near the Cloisters. He was streetwise, which was helpful in dealing with the criminally insane population we worked with at Bellevue.

There was an inmate so violent eight to ten corrections officers were needed to escort him anywhere in the jail system. He was six feet five, 280 pounds of solid muscle, with a black belt in karate who hated correction officers with a passion. Anthony Smith was the most feared man in the correctional system. He had injured dozens of officers during transportation. When he arrived at the Bellevue Hospital bullpen handcuffed, shackled, and a net over his face, Dr. Levine was furious. He had corrections remove all of these restrictions, and Smith was placed in a cell by himself. The officers objected, but Dr. Levine let them know that in a hospital setting, we don't treat patients like animals. The patient never gave us a problem while he was hospitalized. That's the kind of doctor he was, able to resolve all problems with a word and a smile. But if that didn't work, he would pop you in the ass with a needle full of medication. As part of his inner circle staff, I was able to witness firsthand his keen ability to manipulate patients. He wouldn't promise them anything that he couldn't deliver. He wasn't afraid to experiment with medication as long as it benefited the patient. It was a satisfying time for me to work under his tutelage. I learned more under his eight-year leadership than I could ever imagine. I'm not accustomed to showering accolades on a man, but this individual was a real friend of mine. He helped mold me into a better clinician. To this day I'm still thankful for what he brought to the table. He was a class act.

CHAPTER 56

We are genetically designed to enjoy drugs, it's in our DNA. Cocaine is the champagne of drugs and I loved it. But this is not who I was. I was closely monitored, instructed by two beautiful intelligent people. When I was 17 years old I hated everything about my father. The fact that he spoke in broken English with a Latin accent was embarrassing to me. I loathe the way he dressed always in suits with suspenders and corny hats. And that salsa music he played every day drove me crazy. He was always complaining that he was busting his balls working night and day to put rice and beans on the table. He interfered with my social life wouldn't let me stay out past 10 o'clock I felt like a child. I grew up in the lower East side of Manhattan 7th Street Ave. C, alphabet city. In the late 1950s on through the 1960s drugs, alcoholism, prostitution was rampant and to top that off they were burning down the buildings for insurance. I had to get out of there. I began applying to colleges as far away from the Lower East side as possible.

Everybody in my family was into business. My father was a veteran of both World War II and the Korean War. He spent nearly thirteen years in the army before being shot three times in the back in the jungles of Korea. While convalescing at the Fort Hamilton Hospital, in Brooklyn, he was given some financial advice. He was told to take his GI Bill and buy property. He bought himself a multiunit building with a storefront and opened a bodega. In the basement he ran a cockfighting ring. It was part of his cultural heritage. Some of the baby chicks sired by champion roosters could cost as much as $10,000. He went on to buy a couple of buildings and, along with my uncles, opened up a slew of bodegas. He also got into the numbers racket. My mother was a card shark who would drag me to her games as protection. Win or lose she would always give me a couple of dollars. I had an uncle who ran and owned a gay nightclub called La Cueva and a Laundromat. Another uncle owned a bakery shop. I was passed around like an indentured servant. I was a regular handy Andy whether restocking shelves, taking clothes out of washing machines, or being a waiter at the club. There was always something for me to do. After all that was done, I had to do my schoolwork, no time for play. This is why I wanted to get as far away as I could from them. They treated me like their personal slave.

At the time I was unable to see the big picture that this training would be beneficial for me in the long run. I decided to attend Plattsburgh State University, nearly four hundred miles away from the Loisaida, as it is known today. That summer, before heading north to my new digs, I refused to work in their establishments. I was going to take it easy all summer and prepare for my great escape from all of this nonsense.

There was talk of a major concert somewhere in Woodstock. I wanted to go. I wanted to see Carlos Santana, Jimi Hendrix, Canned Heat. I was rebelling against everything that was my parents.

CHAPTER 57

Two days after getting to Plattsburgh, a young girl asked me if I wanted to go to the party. I wasn't sure what she meant. She said it was the incoming freshman class party.

We made plans to meet at the country club where the party was to take place. As I was entering the area where the concert was to be staged, there were a dozen kegs of beer. The entrance fee was a dollar for all you could drink. I then had an epiphany. I heard my father's voice tell me to be careful. I was momentarily spooked. I felt like he was watching my every move.

As I started to hand over my dollar, Diana, the girl that invited me to the shindig, said I didn't have to pay. She said this country club belonged to her father and we were going to go to her room upstairs first. Every hair on my body stood up. I was going to get laid. I sat in a large bean bag chair and made myself comfortable. She then handed me a large flask of Mateus wine to open. During my college days, that was a very popular wine. It showed you were sophisticated.

I uncorked the vino and proceeded to pour her and myself a glass of grapes. I felt anxious with anticipation. She then pulled out a double bamboo marijuana cigarette from her purse and lit it with a wooden matchstick that was three inches long. It was another fashion statement she was making with those matches. The aroma quickly filled the room. I've never smoked marijuana, and I became paranoid that we would be caught by police. But I knew that if I didn't smoke that large, fat rolled up joint with her I wouldn't get the piece of ass I was anticipating. So when she began to pass the joint to me, I took a quick toke and passed it back. In the meantime I continued to drink my wine as if nothing happened. She again started to pass the joint to me, I took another toke and gave it back. I heard my father's voice again and knew he was concerned about me. After finishing half the flask of wine and smoking the joint, I was so stoned I fell out for an hour. When I woke up we did the wild thing and went to the concert.

Even now after so many decades removed from that night, I can still hear my father's voice warning me about impending danger.

I learned one thing that night, that I loved marijuana. The next day I bought an ounce of pot with my father's hard-earned cash, a slap to his face.

I often think about my father, mother, brother, sister, and all the energy that was spent to get me to where I am today. Even when I step into Rikers Island or walk on to Bellevue Hospital prison ward, their presence is always with me. It's my personal reminder that I work in a very dangerous environment. The violence is so intense in both of these facilities that nearly on a daily basis you see slashing and beat-downs, and just last week a correction officer was raped. I've become desensitized to all the mayhem, but I always keep my eyes open to the danger surrounding me. The problem with these institutions is not the inmates or patients. It's the mismanagement by people who lack the proper credentials. How do these individuals, without the proper training, get to gain so much power? It appears that they are attracted to the money and greed. You don't need to have leadership qualities in order to chase the money. Win Powerball or mega lottery and your relatives will come out of the grave looking for you. That's the type of allure money has on people; it will wake up the dead. This is the reason why people position themselves into the role of power; that's where the money will be found. I never had interest in gaining power. My thing was money. But I knew that having money creates a certain side effect, power. If Bill Gates wants to talk to the president of the United States, they will be on the phone within five minutes.

It's like a stage that I'm on when I walk into these places. I've become an actor. I have to make a major performance to convince these individuals that there's a solution to their problems. Addicts are a unique breed. They wake up in the morning with zero dollars in their pockets and within a couple hours they have $100 to spend on drugs. It's amazing how resourceful they can be when it comes to hustling money in order to service their addiction. Every living thing on the planet is a pleasure seeker. From the smallest germ to the largest mammal, we are all looking to be pleased. There are guys who wake up in the morning and need to jerk off three to four times before they can begin their day.

When I began seeing my personal physician, I was sixty-two years old and in pretty good health. I had an old football injury that was acting up, and I went for a checkup. He asked if I was taking any medication. I told him no. He said, "That's unusual. By this time most individuals are taking some sort of medication. How did you do it?" I told him with alcohol, cigarettes, and cocaine. He laughed and said, "Whatever works for you." I hated doctors. They were in the scam business also. Every time I went for a doctor's visit, they wanted to do a battery of tests and charge the insurance companies. Let's face it, doctors and lawyers run this country. Doctors have this large money tree inculcated into our national budgetary system that ensures them with a steady cash flow into their coffers. If a doctor gets busted for inappropriate behavior, they usually get a pass. If need be, they can go to another state and start all over again. It's a very convenient system for them. If inadvertently someone dies under their care, they just bury the body, no questions asked. Lawyers have a similar type of freedom. If you look at the United States Senate, you'll find that 100 percent of the individuals that sit in that system are lawyers. They have an ulterior motive, to protect their profession.

Money is the only language lawyers understand. These lawyers/politicians are in the front line of corruption in America. It is filtered down to every political crony across the country. New York City is just a microcosm of this insidious political behavior. What is the solution to rid this ingrained political infrastructure? Thomas Jefferson once said there should be a revolution every twenty years in order to get rid of the old, complacent blood running the system. Even George Washington knew that it was necessary to have a two-term elected presidency rather than have a lifetime control of the country. He wanted to avoid being labeled a dictator or king. These founding fathers were philosophical and political geniuses. I would think the best thing to do with these political hacks is to line them up in front of a firing squad.

Privatization is not a perfect system, but it does have better controls. It's human nature to always look for the loopholes and cracks in the armor and gain an advantage. This cavalcade of clowns that runs Albany and the New York City government should be held accountable for their actions. You know there's something terribly wrong when New York City spends billions of dollars on the educational system and their product is in the bottom of the totem pole. Of course this all can't be blamed on corruption, but it plays a major role in the failure of our schools. Just take a look at the graduation rate of private schools, and you'll see big differences between the two.

The company I work for at Rikers Island is managed by a private industry. Within one year five mental health aides have been fired for sleeping on the job. There's no review or suspension, just termination. This ensures that others perform their duties to the required standards. Catch a public servant sleeping, such as a corrections officer, and he'll get ten days without pay, but he'll keep his job. What's the difference between these individuals who failed in performing their duties while at work? Unions, they are a powerful group in New York City politics. Private entities are less likely to be stonewalled by unions.

CHAPTER 58

I knew Mr. Serrano would come knocking at my door one day. He wasn't satisfied with my production. He asked me to meet him at Franklin Delano Roosevelt Park in upstate New York for a Fourth of July barbecue. I had an idea of what he wanted, and I was afraid that I wouldn't be able to comply with his wishes. It was a two-hour drive to that park, and I found him sitting in a chaise lounge surrounded by his entourage. You could immediately tell they were from the city. They didn't know how to blend into the environment. They looked like a bunch of spics who just came off a banana boat. They dressed in plaid shirts and pants, with pointy shoes and greasy hair. I thought I was watching a rendition of *West Side Story*.

As was usually the case with Mr. Serrano, his banquet was opulent. I had been to a couple of his fiestas before, and they were always the same, enough food to choke a herd of elephant, all the booze you can drink, and salsa music blasting in the background. There was *lechon asado*, fried chicken, large bloody steaks, and of course, rice and *gandules*, the old Puerto Rican staple. I felt like I was in the Puerto Rican day parade in Central Park in New York City. What would be a party without women? They were all over the place in scanty outfits, tempting every motherfucker there. I saw more hard-ons that day than I've ever seen in my lifetime. Mr. Serrano told me to enjoy the day, that we would talk later. He told me that any lady here was at my beck and call. Mr. Serrano had no idea who I was. Even after spending nearly seven years robbing my back pocket, he still thought I would be impressed with a bunch of whores. I don't do casual sex with anybody and definitely not with prostitutes. Not to mention all the diseases that they carry. Just being near them made me feel leery. A piece of ass could be found anywhere. I had my fill of pussy decades ago when I was a young whippersnapper hanging out in nightclubs. When you begin to mellow out, you look for friends, not one-night stands. At my age spiritual friends are hard to find. There's always an ulterior motive. Women learn not to give their pussy away for free. Most come with some sort of emotional baggage attached to them, and they expect you to solve all these problems. I'm glad I found my spiritual partner a long time ago. She and I have had a great life together.

The fiesta was beginning to wind down, and Mr. Serrano called me over. He asked how I was doing. I told him everything was all right. He was interested to know why the money was short. I told him things had changed at Bellevue dramatically. I told him the proliferation of cameras throughout the hospital made it difficult to run business as usual. Everyone, everything was being closely monitored, watched, and recorded. And the old-timers were the primary targets. It had gotten so difficult to do business that I stopped bringing in the jewelry. It was too bulky, conspicuous, and easily seen by the bubbles in the sky. I told him I couldn't afford to lose my job. I still needed it to maintain my family. Besides, I wasn't running after the dollar as hard as I used to when I was in my early twenties. He then had the audacity to ask me about Rikers Island and the potential for doing business there. That is when I knew I had to get rid of Mr. Serrano. He was an unbearable burden to my business. I was going to start strategizing on how to get rid of this motherfucker from my life. I had no choice but to kill him. There's only one problem with this type of organization. Killing Mr. Serrano would mean just changing bosses. They have an uncanny ability to grow another head. Someone else would take his place. I wasn't sure if murdering him would solve my problem.

I tried to reason with Mr. Serrano concerning Rikers Island, that there were a confluence of factors why venturing into Rikers Island to do business was not a good idea. He didn't listen. He insisted that I make an attempt at making money on the Rock. I told him I was not going to do it, that they were too many eyes, too many ears, and too much security to take such a risk. He said he would be traveling to Puerto Rico for two months. He would like to see a plan when he got back.

The only plan I was going to be working on was how to murder that motherfucker. He didn't give a fuck about me. All he cared about was the bottom line. Either way, I was going to get fucked by Mr. Serrano. I spent too many years building my reputation at Rikers to let a guy like this put me in such a predicament. What was the nobler thing to do, ice Mr. Serrano or lose my reputation at Rikers? My street credit would be enhanced by killing that bloodsucker who would continue to torment me with his irrational demands.

CHAPTER 59

The administration in my department began to float me more into the detox unit. Many of the patients in this unit had a similar history of incarceration and mental illness. They wanted me to develop a motivational group dealing with the personal issues that brought people to addiction. Anything that would help me diversify my résumé was welcomed.

When I was first moved to detox, the average length of stay was one to two weeks. It was later shortened to three to five days for economic reasons. The insurance companies refused to pay for more than five days. It was the new economic reality facing our hospital. It cost $1,500 a day to be treated in this unit, not counting any additional battery of tests that may have to be performed on the patient, such as abdominal ultrasound, medical consult, x-ray, which would be an added cost that can balloon the bill of a client/patient hospital stay to well over $10,000.

On the average, 170 to 180 patients are treated by this service per month. And what do we get in return for this exorbitant amount of money? Not much. Some individuals when they leave our unit run into the bathroom and shoot a bag of dope. Others go looking for the quart of vodka they stashed in the park. Such was the case with one of our client/patient who kept getting up to look out the window during our verbal motivational group. I had to know what was going on. Why was he so intent on looking out the window? It turned out he had hidden a bottle of vodka in the bushes while waiting to get into detox.

I assured him that bottle was gone. With all the bums living in the park, they would have spotted it by now. Another guy came in strung out on K2. For three days he didn't even know his name or where he was staying. He began to come out of the stupor and was now in better control of his mental faculties. He decided it was time to go. So he packed his bags, stripped his bed, and got ready to leave. Frantically he searched through his bags and finally asked the staff who stole his K2. He was not aware that contraband, by law, had to be flushed down the toilet. He threw a conniption upon learning we had thrown it out. This is the distorted thinking produced by addiction. K2 has become one of the most dangerous drugs being abused by our children. Eleven-year-old kids are smoking it. It has reached epidemic stages, and there is no end in sight. It's cheap, readily available, and legal. There's no stopping this scourge.

This is not an isolated case. Most of the individuals that come into our detox struggle with rational thinking. They tend to embrace abnormal behavioral patterns in order to achieve comfort. Negative consequences can easily be justified with an "I don't give a fuck" attitude.

Dealing with these addicts helped me understand myself a little better. I spent a forty-two-year career working with criminals, addicts, and discarded children. There is no book you could read that will explain how to deal with this unique population. You have to be spectacular, phenomenal to work with these individuals. You can't disguise who you are. They can see right through your facade. You learn to buck the tide. It's suicidal to walk into these places and think you are in control. I discovered all this emotional duress can be detrimental to your health. You become part of the group. It's a jolt of electricity when you become part of this spectrum. I was never planning anything; it was all spontaneous. Everything was against the rules. There was a certain freedom I felt being involved with these caricatures. They allowed me to enter this world.

No matter how long you work with this population, there's always something new to be learned.

The guy who killed his father over a reduction in his allowance never wanted to talk to me. Here's a person who injected himself with steroids in order to look muscled. His father was worth millions of dollars; he was part of the privileged class. And now he finds himself in a mental observation area hoping to be found not guilty by reason of insanity. White males are always part of a culture that are hated by minorities. Few are able to survive this intense beat-down. The physical and mental obstacles really do not matter, they will be destroyed by this violent culture.

I got over with girls, women who always try to nurture me. They always wanted to help me with their wisdom. I was at a jazz club in Montreal, the capital of jazz music at the time. I was twenty years old and trying to find myself.

I had already been to the great concert of Woodstock, seen the landing on the moon, escaped participating in the Vietnam War, and managed to hitchhike across the country. When you're eighteen years old, nothing seems to get in your way.

Working with the criminal mind was fascinating. Whenever I would go to any type of gathering, it was a showstopper. If anyone found out that I worked with the criminally insane at both Rikers Island and Bellevue Hospital, I would be the center of attention. Instantly I had a captivated audience peppering me with an endless number of questions. Aside from entertaining them with some of the horror stories, I also had put together some comical routines in order to provide some levity to my audience.

John Monroe was the nastiest individual I've ever met in the criminal justice system. He had been arrested for inflicting well over three hundred stitches across the face of a doctor treating his daughter for a rare disease. She was twelve years old when she passed away. John Monroe wanted to talk with the doctor. He wanted to inquire about what went wrong, but the doctor refused to provide any details. Mr. Monroe jumped across the desk and began slashing his face with a razor. The pictures that I saw were horrible. The cartilage of his nose was completely severed, and one eye was punctured. The scene was so gruesome I nearly vomited. That was his modus operandi. He slashed over a dozen detainees at Rikers.

While awaiting trial on an attempted homicide case, the judge made him a final offer. He came over to me crying. I asked him what happened? The judge wanted to give him twelve years. He said he could do ten, but he couldn't do twelve. That's the sort of get-over mentality these individuals display at all times. He was a Houdini. No matter how thorough they searched him, they were unable to find his weapon of choice, razors. I admired his ability to confound the system. It didn't matter how many years the judge gave him. Two weeks after arriving at the prison upstate, he was murdered by one of the guys he slashed.

Life in jail or prison is cheap. Anyone could be victimized, and John Monroe paid the ultimate price for his behavior.

I am not supposed to pass judgment, but John Monroe was an asshole who deserved every fucking thing that happened to him. He was a horrible person with no redeeming qualities. He tried to cut Dr. Flynn and Barbara Allen, the administrator at Bellevue prison ward. He was an angry individual.

CHAPTER 60

Dr. Stern, who was the spitting image of Carly Simon, the songstress, had a violent encounter with one of our patients. He picked up a Bic pen that was lying on top of a table in the conference room where she was interviewing this guy. Before she could react, he had stabbed her several times about the face. Her screams echoed across the hallways of our unit. When we arrived at the scene, she was a bloody mess. This was long before the HIPAA laws of confidentiality were implemented. She had insisted to meet privately with the patient, big mistake. Dr. Stern was scarred for life both physically and mentally. She had recently gotten married to a multimillionaire philanthropist and was enjoying her honeymoon. This assault devastated the relationship between them. She wanted to continue to be a doctor; he had other ideas. Dr. Stern returned to work for a few days but was unable to overcome this devastating blow to her psyche. She acquiesced to her husband's demands and never came back. The pretrial detainee never had anything to lose; his life continued as usual. He was already facing twenty-five to life for multiple bodies. This is the danger you face when you are working with a population who doesn't give a fuck. Whose life is next to be destroyed or impacted by this irrational behavior? Dr. Stern and her beau returned to Arkansas, where she started a family. Over the years she called me a few times, but eventually we lost contact. I admired the good doctor for trying to come back and work with these assholes.

You learn to depend on your primal instincts to remain safe, which is your number one priority. The violence at Rikers Island and Bellevue Hospital is so intense and taxing on your psyche that it took me nearly four years to feel somewhat comfortable. You have to constantly be adjusting your thinking. When you witness slashings and beat-downs, you can't help but be affected by this extreme behavior. Strange as it may sound, I love being part of this mix. I wake up at five o'clock in the morning knowing I would be entering this dark world. It'll be 10:30 p.m. by the time I get home. For nearly seventy hours per week, Monday through Saturday, I'm in direct proximity with this population, and I love it. Sometimes I wonder if there's something wrong with me to feel so passionate about my career choice. To feel so at ease working in such a hostile atmosphere. It feels like an out-of-body experience, a dream with no ending. Perhaps I am just crazy, and this is a menagerie set up to keep me trapped in an odd world. I can't help but question my mental stability. Whether this is actual reality or a figment of my imagination intertwined in a cruel joke. I often tremble when I think I'm part of an experimentation set up to be studied like a lab rat. If you look at my track record of drug dealing, loan sharking, gunrunning, and ambulance chasing, the law of karma should've dealt me a tragic blow by now.

I've had a few close calls with the police. I picked up three and a half grams of cocaine for delivery to a Rikers Island administrator. She's what we call in the business a cocaine whore. She was being passed around by two psychiatrists, and they would buy her drugs. I always kept half a gram for myself as partial payment. I asked her to meet me at a prearranged destination, and I handed over three grams of 97 percent pure cocaine. I wasn't aware that I was being observed by a team of undercover narcotic agents. I then got into my Toyota Echo and drove off toward Rikers Island. They surrounded my car and told me to get out. One officer said, "You're in big trouble." I always placed the half gram in my mouth just in case I was stopped by the police. I bit the plastic bag and swallowed it. They ransacked my car, but they found nothing. They wanted to know who the woman was in the black Explorer. I told them I worked with her in Rikers Island. They told me to get out of there, and off I went back into the Rock. When that cocaine melted into my system, I had a splitting headache.

I was on my way to Bellevue Hospital one Saturday morning when I ran a red light. There was an ounce of cocaine and several guns underneath the passenger's seat. If this contraband was found in my car, I could easily be facing fifteen to twenty years in prison. The sirens were blaring, and the lights were flashing. He called out over his megaphone to pull over. I became very nervous. I had to regain my composure before he got to my driver's side window. If I didn't gain control, he would want to search my car. He asked me for my license and registration. He said I was speeding and ran a red light. I had the gall to ask him for professional courtesy. He wanted to know what I did. I told him I worked at Rikers Island. He asked if I was an officer. Therapist, I told him. "Then you don't get professional courtesy, you're not on the job." He told me he would give me one ticket for running a red light, and I felt fortunate. I believe the placard I had on the dashboard of my car saved me from getting busted.

It's impossible to account for every variable when it comes to unscrupulous business practices. You have sleazeballs trying to rob your money, cops trying to bust you, and women willing to fuck you for cash. That's what you call a trifecta. The end result is that you have a looming target strapped to your back and a multitude of people willing to shoot you. Anytime I walked out of Bellevue Hospital, I would always have my head turning in all directions. I never stop to chitchat with anybody. It was too dangerous, especially for the next four to five days after the pay period. It was not a big secret that at this time I would carry large sums of money; people knew. I feared they would crack my head open if given the opportunity. I could always make money. It's being left physically debilitated that concerned me more than anything else. Some of these feelings of paranoia would at times paralyze me.

CHAPTER 61

Psychiatry has turned into this alternative lifestyle due to the pursuit of drugs by these individuals. In the mid-1980s, I ran into a Bellevue Hospital psychiatrist who was picking up homosexuals at two o'clock in the morning at Jackson Heights, Queens. A doctor who worked at Bellevue prison ward. This was in the midst of the AIDS epidemic when no reputable psychiatrist wanted to be associated with the gay community for fear that they might lose their private practice. He was cruising in one of the most notorious gay areas in that borough. I was shocked to see him driving around in his black rental Ford Accord. He had stopped in front of me to pick up a passenger. When he saw me standing no more than five feet away from him, he stepped on the gas and sped off into the night. The next time I saw Dr. Miller, he couldn't look me in the eyes.

Dr. Miller originated from a small town in Arkansas. Many individuals with alternative lifestyle flock to the Big Apple searching for anonymity and freedom to explore their sexuality. Little hamlets in rural America back in the early '80s cramped Dr. Miller's sexual dreams. He left Bellevue a few years later never to be heard from again.

I began strategizing on how to deal with Mr. Serrano. He had become a huge burden on my mind, an impediment to my continued success, and he was back from Puerto Rico. My options were limited. But I had to do something about this albatross around my neck. I knew from my prior experience with Rikers Island inmates that people always talk. They rat each other out when it's beneficial, when there is something to be gained. Someone's always trying to get the upper hand. I wondered what price I would have to pay for this deed, to murder Mr. Serrano.

At Rikers, an inmate told me the best candidate to carry out a slashing was the guy who had nothing to lose. Someone with multiple bodies, no bail, and who is facing life without parole would be selected to commit the crimes, what they call a lifer.

Or you could choose a guy who's been in and out of jail or prison for the last thirty-five years. They are so institutionalized they don't know how to live in the outside world, so it's inevitable that they will be arrested again.

The Latin Kings would help me out. I knew a major player in this gang. He always looked forward to my therapeutic interventions. We would spend two to three hours per week discussing his personal issues. He felt comfortable enough to release all of his emotional baggage during these sessions. I could arrange an assassination with his help. He was a high-ranking Latin King who had connections outside the four walls of Rikers.

At first I was hesitant to approach him. It's difficult to go into this sort of relationship with an inmate who has no heart. This could morph into a precarious web where there would be no going back to a normal life. My personal freedom was at stake. I began to quiz him about his ability to get things done outside Rikers Island.

He was grandiose and bragging about all the things that he had accomplished outside Rikers. In the Latin King organization, he was considered a general. Whenever I visited his unit, all deals went through him. There was no disputing that he was in charge. He even had control of the corrupt officers.

You could see he enjoyed the spotlight. Nothing went on in that unit without his approval. The power he wheeled was impressive, but would it translate to doing business outside the Rock?

I began a fishing expedition geared at finding out everything about his outside business. He had an elaborate verbal code to communicate with the home front. His wife, a Latin queen, ran the operation from a duplex apartment situated in the northern part of the Bronx. She would pass on the messages to a network controlled by a hierarchy of personnel he governed. Drug dealing, extortion, loan sharking, and of course, Murder Inc. were all part of the domain he ran to make money.

Other than murder for hire, him and I were not that much different. We both ran an enterprise of nefarious activities to make money. I was one small mistake away from facing 25 to life and sharing a bunk with this guy. But Mr. Serrano's immense pressure to expand my business dealing into Rikers Island gave me no choice. I had to eliminate him by any means necessary. I decided to make an alliance with Hector's crew.

During our therapeutic session I began to manipulate Hector in order to finalize my plan of purging Mr. Serrano from my life. Getting to Mr. Serrano was going to be a difficult task. His headquarters was located up in Spanish Harlem and he was heavily guarded by a slew of henchmen who monitor his every move. I wasn't concerned about the logistics of the plan. My job was to pay Hector off after its completion. I was vacillating whether to use Hector to ice Mr. Serrano.

Without giving away my secret intentions, during our therapy sessions, I asked him how much a kilo of cocaine would sell for in the streets of New York. The price he quoted was in the same range that I bought my merchandise. I had to be subtle with my questions. He wasn't a stupid guy. This inmate was running a major crime syndicate from behind Rikers Island. I had to be careful not to expose my ulterior motive. I had to be sure that he would accept my request of murdering Mr. Serrano without questions. These therapeutic sessions went unabated for a couple of weeks before I was able to generate enough nerve to ask him how much it would cost to murder somebody. He was on to me. I felt like he saw right through me. He said it depends on who you wanted killed. He said every murder commands a different price.

It felt like I was in a car dealership looking for the best price. I really didn't want to pay for a Mercedes-Benz when a Toyota Corolla would suffice. In one of our therapeutic sessions, he bluntly asked me what I was looking for and to be honest with him. I told him I wanted to kill Louis Serrano, who had been badgering me for months to conduct business on Rikers Island. The mention of Louis Serrano's name seemed to baffle Hector. I could see that he was taken aback when I brought up his name. Mr. Serrano was synonymous with the Neta gang fellowship. They were rival groups who hated each other with a passion. Hector wanted to know how I knew Mr. Serrano. It wasn't till then that I got to understand how powerful Mr. Serrano really was in his community. I had placed Hector in a conundrum. By the mobster's code of ethics, Mr. Serrano was virtually insulated from assassination attempts on his life. A fail-safe way of maintaining the peace between these organizations. The murder of Mr. Serrano could spark an all-out war between these factions. But when you're running shit from behind bars, you don't give a fuck about the consequences. Besides, he was trying to impress me with his ability to get things done while locked up in Rikers. He told me that to kill somebody of his stature and reputation would easily cost $100,000. He then offered me a discount. He would cut the cost of this business transaction in half, since he didn't like that motherfucker anyway. I needed to know if they would be any added demands down the road on his behalf. "I never take anything off the table until my belly is full, but I'll make an exception for you. $50,000 is my price and our contract is done, no strings attached." It seemed as though Hector had his own agenda with this group.

I would make my decision within a few weeks and get back to him. My other option was Hakeem and his crew. They seemed reckless enough to take on this type of project. I hadn't seen Hakeem for over five years. We lost contact soon after I stopped supplying him with guns and cigarettes from South Carolina. He had made his own connections and didn't need me anymore. I tried calling him, but his phone had been disconnected. The only way to get in contact with him would be to go to that dreaded project he lived in. It wasn't logistically feasible to expand my search for a killer that would murder Mr. Serrano. You can't trust anybody in the business of murder. They will give you up in a minute for a better deal. Later on when I tried to get in touch with Hakeem, he had been pumped with fifteen rounds in a drive-by. I made up my mind to go with Hector, no sense in looking for anybody else; it was too risky.

During our next therapeutic session, I gave Hector the go-ahead. He told me I needed to give his wife a 50 percent down payment to get the show started. The rest of the money would be delivered upon the completion of the job. "If you renege on the final payment, we will come after you." He said that if I change my mind, I would forfeit the down payment. He assured me that the job would get done but extensive planning needed to be made before an assassination could be carried out. He would give me instructions on where and when to meet his wife, Juanita.

My body felt numb as though I was bitten by a king cobra and the venom was circulating throughout my bloodstream, sucking the life out of me. It's a strange feeling to order somebody killed. But I didn't feel the guilt I was expecting. I guess Mr. Serrano's evil intentions justified my action. I was never the type of guy that would stand by and let myself be abused by anyone. It was not in my DNA. Mr. Serrano's insistence that I create a business at Rikers Island went against my moral values. Although I was running an evil empire at Bellevue Hospital, it was of my own volition. Mr. Serrano's strong-arm tactics did not sit well with me.

Mr. Serrano was a fat, greedy maricon who always had a cigar in his mouth. He wanted to put my freedom in danger by telling me to go into Rikers Island to sell drugs and alcohol. I told him, "The risk was not worth taking the chance, and security is tightening up even more nowadays."

He asked me, "Is it impossible to smuggle something in there?" He looked me straight in my eyes and asked again, "Is it impossible?" He tried to be intimidating by raising his voice. "Let's face it, every day I read in the newspaper and hear in the local news how Rikers Island is so porous and security so lax that someone, a correction officer no less, was able to smuggle in there a loaded gun," he stated as though he was an expert on security matters at Rikers Island. Guys like him always make me laugh. They think they know everything. They know very little jack shit about what goes on in a place like this.

I said to him, "Listen, you have to weigh these things out. What's in the best interest of your company? Is me getting busted the best thing that could happen for your company?"

He appeared defenseless, unable to respond to what I just said. He took a long toke on his cigar, and for a few moments we just sat there not saying a word. After gathering his thoughts again, he began rambling on about the potential of doing business at Rikers. He was obsessed with the place. Every time we had a meeting, that's all he would talk about. How Rikers Island's potential was being wasted. "Why don't you try doing it on a small scale first and then see how that works?" he suggested.

"How do you think I should do this, bring in a bag of dope or have a half pint of Bacardi? Is that small enough for you?" I replied in a condescending way.

"Don't get smart," he shot back angrily. I could tell he was frustrated by my defiance.

"What if I get busted? Are you going to be there to bail me out, hire lawyers that will help me beat this case?" I asked. "It's easy for you to sit back and give orders, but it's my butt that would be on the line, not yours," I yelled at him.

He told me, "Calm down, sleep on it, think it over. If there's a possibility that this could be done, it would be great."

CHAPTER 62

Teresa was a single mom raising two teenage girls and was barely making ends meet. I always had a soft spot for women struggling to raise their kids. On numerous occasions I would give her a couple of dollars so she could buy the daughters a few things. It was a way for me to keep my moral compass pointing in the right direction. At times she would invite me over to her office to eat lunch that she had brought from home. It was during one of these moments that she began to take off her blouse. I asked her what she was doing. She wanted to reward my kind heart. "You don't owe me anything, I gave the money to your daughters. If you needed to use the money for something else, that's on you." She told me I was a class act and thanked me for being sweet. Bellevue Hospital is full of women with the same problem, and I feel sorry for them.

I was now in the process of meeting up with Hector for another session and to get instructions on how to proceed. He wanted me to drive to Mohegan Sun casino in Connecticut with a backpack full of the money. I was to meet up there with Juanita. He told me that there was no time clock to complete the assassination.

I decided to take a vacation. Go see the Inca ruins of Peru. I had to give my brain a break, try to distance myself from this whole convoluted nightmare that was now interfering with every aspect of my life. The pressure was becoming unbearable. I could hardly think straight.

For a few days I had to escape the madness surrounding me. I was unable to get away from my conscience. You could travel to a bucolic oasis in the middle of paradise, but you can't exorcise your inner demons. They come along for the ride. After landing in Lima, Peru, I went to a local cantina and had a coca tea drink, a traditional Indian beverage made from the coca leaf. For the next seven days I drank enough of this hallucinogenic concoction to forget New York City altogether. For a brief moment I contemplated not going back to the hustle and bustle of New York.

No matter how far I would go to recharge my batteries, coming back home always made me feel fantastic. There is something special about New York City that you can't find anywhere else in the world. I've been to Rome, Paris, Athens, and a slew of other large cities around the world. New York is the only place where you can get up at three o'clock in the morning and buy a ham-and-cheese sandwich. There are places where you could buy a bag of dope easier than purchase milk for your baby. This is the ambiance that I loved about New York City, the pleasure capital of the world.

Soon after landing at Kennedy International Airport, I called Juanita to arrange our meeting. It was a rainy Sunday afternoon, and I-95 was packed with traffic. Due to all the accidents, it took me nearly three hours to get there. Juanita was a tall dark-haired beauty. She was a superstar model type. Hector often bragged about how beautiful she was, and he was right. Everything about her was gorgeous, even her personality. We spent a few hours playing at the roulette table before renting a room where we completed our transaction.

CHAPTER 63

Anita Brown, a close friend, was complaining about corruption in the system. How it doesn't allow you to move up through promotion. She was applying for a position at Gouverneur Hospital and was afraid she would be turned down because of the nepotism practice taking place there. Despite the fact that Anita was the most qualified applicant, she could easily be bumped by some family member. Incompetent individuals who are not even credentialed to perform the job they are given. All city and state agencies have this corruption embedded into the system. Politicians are the number one culprits abusing the system for financial gain. And little persons likes Anita, who makes $37,000 a year as a secretary, can only steal paperclips.

I was informed by a coworker that before the implementation of checks and balances by the nursing administration, overtime was being abused at a phenomenal rate. You could be on vacation, out of town, or in another country. All you had to do was X the timesheet in and out, code it, forge a supervisor's initials, submit to payroll, and you'll get paid. Today a stack of papers has to be filled out and be preapproved in order for anyone to do overtime. But loopholes are still out there waiting for some genius to take advantage. It's just a matter of time before they exploit them. There are dozens of departments at Bellevue and thousands of time sheets floating throughout the hospital. I've known a few timekeepers, and they've explained the inherent corruption locked into this system. Over the years, millions have been stolen. Recently, a coordinating manager with significant knowledge of the inner workings of this system acknowledged to me that she had been stealing time for decades. Not a large amount, $40 to $60 per pay period, enough to keep her in cigarettes and beer all this time. There was no remorse on her part. She saw an opportunity and took it. Just like anyone else who is giving this amount of control over an item that can produce cash. Now you have to give the nursing administration some props for putting in place mechanisms to reduce this kind of corruption.

Anita was a thick, chubby, light-skinned African American woman with a face full of freckles whom I knew well over a decade, and she always had me in stitches with her sarcastic humor. She was a dope fiend who was always nodding out when we went to hang out and smoke cigarettes. I knew she had a big problem, but I never tried to address it with her. She was constantly borrowing money to service her addiction.

One day while she was trying to hustle one of the clinicians for cash, I told her, "Get your act together, Anita."

She had a conniption and went into a verbal rage. "What the fuck are you trying to say, Rubildo? Please don't get into my personal business, I don't appreciate it." She continued her verbal barrage unabated. "What about the shit you pull around here? Be careful what you say about me. I know what you do around here."

This was the first and only time I tried to broach the subject matter about her addiction. I stopped hanging out with her for a long period of time, gave her room to calm down. I didn't want to retaliate against her. She had a lot of issues, mainly financial.

Within a matter of a few weeks, she came looking to apologize.

"Rubildo, I was out of line a couple weeks back, I would like to apologize," she said in a low voice. "I know you just trying to look out for me, my bad."

I couldn't stay angry at her, so I told her, "No problem, don't worry."

But our relationship was never the same again. I could be very vindictive at times. Once you crossed me, I'm done with you. I had trained myself to be leery of people, and her threats didn't sit well with me.

Every year Bellevue purchases 25 turkeys for the patient's Thanksgiving holiday dinners and by the time these turkeys had landed in the twelfth-floor cafeteria, four birds had taken flight to unknown destinations. Most likely they are flying around in Spanish Harlem or the South Bronx, any place within the five boroughs of New York City or even New Jersey. This was a ritual that took place not only on Thanksgiving but also on Christmas, New Year's, Father's Day, Mother's Day, and Easter Sunday.

Ironically, this same individual who was pilfering Bellevue's cargo walked around with a Bible, reading religious quotes from the good book.

She would strut past hospital security with gallons of Benjamin Moore paint and claim the painters gave them to her.

There were pharmacists who owned businesses ripping off large jars of medication from Bellevue. Ibuprofen and Naprosyn were medications that were being tested at Bellevue Hospital at the time. They were nonsteroidal, anti-inflammatory medications to relieve pain.

Mike Russo gave me the breakdown on these medications. He said, "If the FDA approves ibuprofen and Naprosyn, these pharmaceutical companies stand to make billions. If you have a couple of expendable dollars, buy all the shares you can, it will make you a huge profit."

I was not able to make this sort of investment at this time. I didn't have the money.

Mike came from a well-to-do family. They owned a few properties in the West Village, a couple of buildings that generated huge income.

Mike had lost his right eye while playing with a rope keychain he kept swinging back and forth in a circular motion.

His eye cracked like an egg ready to be fried in a skillet. Fluids drained from the socket. It was a mess according to his description.

When you are making minimum wage, you will steal anything at your workplace. Bellevue Hospital is vulnerable to these predators.

Bellevue Hospital and Rikers Island, mega facilities with budgets so large they rival some small islands in the Pacific. One person cannot manage these facilities alone. The MTA is the monster of corruption run by individuals who have never set foot inside a subway or bus. They ride around in chauffeur-driven limousines and have no concept of the struggle an average Joe goes through in his daily commute. They receive exorbitant salaries, incredible perks, and are always crying poverty. This is why I continue to run these elicit, profitable activities at Bellevue. If they could pilfer this incredible amount of moola and get a slap on the wrist, then I'm going to take my chances.

A quarter of Bellevue Hospital staff should be in prison today for what they did during Hurricane Sandy. They stole everything—computers, furniture, copper wiring, equipment—and above all else, they stole the almighty dollar by forging the time sheets. The only thing that survived this onslaught was the chapel cross. I'm surprised they didn't steal the nails holding up Jesus Christ.

I'm provided a budget of $200 to buy supplies for my program. There are numerous ways I could manipulate this money so I can steal some of it without anyone knowing. But this is chump change, not worth my effort. In fact over the last thirty years I've donated a significant amount of money to run the program. Perhaps it's my guilty conscience trying to make amends. It takes millions to run

Bellevue Hospital with hundreds of budgets allocated to different departments. The $200 they give me ranks near or at the bottom of the totem pole. Other departments worked with hundreds of thousands of dollars, even millions. The nurses' budget has always been a hotbed of corruption.

Rikers Island continues to be a magnet for morons who want to make big bucks by sneaking in drugs and alcohol contraband. The latest *stupido* was a male nurse who thought he had devised perfection. They all think their scheme is unique, free of detection. He would put alcohol in vials and buried them in pork fried rice from the local Chinese takeout joints. Marijuana, heroin, and cocaine would be stored in wonton soup in order to pass it into the facility. But IG, the intelligence gathering department, at our jail was reviewing images gathered by a magna meter, a sophisticated imaging device, an x-ray machine that could see through this scheme. He had been doing this for years. The IG suspected him of wrongdoing but were never able to gather enough evidence to charge him. The warden ordered that all food items must pass through the x-ray machine, no exceptions. That would've been my cue to stop this form of trafficking. But when you are making extra money, you get addicted to a certain lifestyle. I heard he had a few condos, a big house, and $85,000 Beamer. When IG correction officers handcuffed him, he began crying like a baby.

CHAPTER 64

There's no statute of limitations on murder. I will have this hanging over my head for the rest of my life. Always having to look over my shoulder would make me feel uncomfortable. I began to have my doubts about murdering Mr. Serrano. All the other things I was doing can get you a slap on the wrist, but with murder, the police will haunt you for life. I had to make a decision soon. Time was running out. I was to meet with Hector at the end of the week. He knew not to do anything until then. He had to get my go-ahead.

When we got together that Friday afternoon, he appeared somewhat animated, excited to talk. He emphasized that we were in the planning stages. It would be awhile before this happened. I told him to take his time, that I hadn't yet decided to kill Mr. Serrano. I told him to keep me abreast of all planning by his crew. I wanted a detailed synopsis of how this was going to take place. The only fear I had now was that Hector was grandiose and always bragging. He's apt to make a mistake and expose the plan. I wondered why I got involved with this man. I began to contemplate packing it all in and walking away. In this business, everything has a price, including retirement. It is also part of a monstrous beast. No Don would want to let go of the money I was producing. They want you to stay creating wealth till death; it's a marriage for life. A lifetime prison term you cannot escape. This is why I wanted to rid myself of Mr. Serrano, who owned the gate keys.

Out of nowhere, Juanita, Hector's beautiful Latin queen, called. She wanted to meet up with me. I had no idea what was on her mind. We agreed to a rendezvous in the Lower East Side of Manhattan, my old stomping ground. We met at a club that had been around for over one hundred years. Initially it was an Irish pub, but the influx of Latino immigrants changed the whole flavor of how business was done. When I arrived, she was sitting in the back sipping on a Cuba libre. She looked elegant, dressed in tight jeans with a flowery blouse and high-heeled black pumps. She had a natural sexual aura about her with a sensual appeal. Men couldn't help but look at her; she was stunning. As I got closer to where she was sitting, her long wavy jet-black hair shined. Her lips, eyes, and nose captivated my imagination. She was pretty as a rose. I was mystified by her request to meet, not knowing what to expect. She greeted me with a hug and kissed my cheek. Her demeanor was subdued as though something was troubling this Latin queen.

The first thing she told me was, "Hector is facing life in prison without the possibility of parole. He's been charged with a double homicide, racketeering, and extortion." She felt it would be ludicrous to wait for him to get out of this predicament. She knew that King Hector was a major fuck-up, a degenerate with no future. He insisted that she wait for him. But the odds were against this marriage now. There was no way this marriage could survive. She was looking for a way out. At first I thought she was looking for my professional help, but I later found out she had an ulterior motive. This queen bee wanted to have a relationship, which could put my life in jeopardy. She wanted out of the life.

Once or twice a week she would travel from the North Bronx by subway to see me for lunch dates. I took her to several restaurants around the Bellevue Hospital area. At Asian cuisine she would always order steamed vegetable dumplings; they were her favorite. At the Waterfront Ale House she preferred French onion soup to go along with a medium-rare hamburger, cutting up the pickle in a meticulous, precise way to be placed on that large Angus piece of meat. Sometimes we would walk down to Starbucks on Twenty-Third Street and First Avenue for a designer cup of joe she cherished. This went on for several weeks before she dropped a bombshell on my lap. She never gave the order to kill Mr. Serrano. She didn't want me to be involved with Hector anymore. Everything and everyone that he comes in contact with is destroyed. She wanted to protect me at all costs. She agreed to return my $25,000 as long as I stayed away from Hector. I made a pact to abide by her wishes.

It was Christmas season, and you could hear caroling in every corner of the city. We had been in contact for nearly five months and eaten every ethnic food known to man. I finally got enough nerve to tell her I wanted to suck her pussy. She blushed but didn't object to my request. In fact, a faint smile of approval appeared across her naked lips. She let me know by her body language that my flirtatious advances were welcomed. This simple act of human interaction between us quenched a thirst in my psyche. I began to make plans with her in mind. She wasn't just a fuck. I wanted to make a full-time commitment and be her partner. She said, "You carry too much baggage, we can talk about it later at another time." I was concerned about what she meant. I had familial obligations, which would interfere with our relationship. This is why she was a class act, willing to give up everything desirable in her life to protect me. I learned a long time ago that women like to fuck; it's all about timing.

Christmas was now a memory, and the new year was right around the corner when she called. She invited me on a Saturday, January 4, to meet up in a hotel room. She was kind of shy stripping down to her panties and bra. I, on the other hand, had an erection before walking into the room. I couldn't take my clothes off fast enough, and seeing my hard-on, she looked away. It revealed an inner part of her that was attractive. This Latin queen who had the power to have men killed was a softy at heart. I encouraged her to relax, that I would never hurt a woman. I quickly removed the fancy underwear she had bought for this occasion and began orally pleasuring her pussy. We spent close to two hours exploring our bodies. That day she became something special to me.

We continued to do the restaurant scene and occasionally sneaked into hotels to ravage each other's body. By now Hector was rotting away in some state prison after being found guilty of murder and extortion. Juanita moved from the Bronx to New Jersey and had no further contact with King Hector. She also lost interest in me, and I have not seen or heard from Juanita for a number of years now. I often think about her and the joy she brought me for a brief moment. Even now I can still smell and taste her feminine essence. She was a unique woman. It hurts me to realize that she will never be a part of my life again. I wasn't prepared to handle such an abrupt ending to our relationship. I hope wherever she is things are all right with her.

CHAPTER 65

The violence at Rikers Island and Bellevue Hospital continues unabated with little relief in sight. There's not one specific reason you could pinpoint for the upsurge of slashing, stabbings, and group violence that permeate throughout these facilities. It's a culmination of a lot of variables that fuels this hostile environment. Crime goes through cycles.

New designer drugs consumed by early adolescence have to top this list. Narcotics such as K2, angel dust, and crack cocaine retard brain development in these young children. It helps them develop an emotional indifference to reality; they lose conscionable remorse to the human experience. Couple that with lack of father figure and you have an angry child who feels neglected and willing to take a risk.

Adolescents by nature are risk takers. They feel bulletproof, invincible, nothing could happen to them. There's a new generation of adolescents waiting to replace these old gangsters, and that's the sad part.

The proliferation of cameras help shut down correctional facility's ability to govern their domain. These cameras and lawsuits place intense pressure on the way correction officers could perform their job.

Detainees quickly learned if a correction officer placed their hands on him, he could sue, not the city of New York, but the officer himself. The cameras handcuffed officers who thought this brand-new tool would be beneficial to them.

Poverty and lack of education is the cornerstone of this problem. A young twelve- or thirteen-year-old adolescent strung out on angel dust at seven thirty in the morning is not going to function normally. Education becomes secondary to his life, then add welfare recipient to the mix and you have a broth of calamity waiting to evolve into violence. Economics plays a role in the overall factor at street-level violence. Danger and death are commonplace behind the walls of Rikers Island and Bellevue Hospital.

You have a layered cake of problems. There's no recovery to mental illness. Chemical intervention only provides limited relief. It's a motivating factor to engage in organized criminal activities. Mental illness is a debilitating disease that can only be kept at bay through chemical intervention, a temporary solution. The solutions are limited unless you want to perform a lobotomy.

The way C 95 is designed, the largest penal colony in the United States, it's nearly impossible to properly manage it. It has structural flaws geared for the detainees to have the upper hand.

The pharmaceutical corporations are a conglomerate of greed and corruption. They are willing to sacrifice every man, woman, and child to addiction in order to maintain a healthy profit margin.

Bellevue Hospital is a bloated conglomerate very difficult to manage; it is too large. It should be broken up into smaller entities.

A year and a half ago Mr. Serrano was gunned down by his enemies. No one ever contacted me concerning paying out protection money. So I'm now free to conduct my business in peace. Only God and a few angels had it better than me, and I'm not sure about the angels.

ABOUT THE AUTHOR

Mr. Rubildo is a Senior Activity Therapist who has worked at both Rikers Island and Bellevue Hospital Forensic Prison ward with the criminally insane. He worked with this population for over four decades. He was the first activity therapist to provide continuity of care for prison inmates at both Rikers Island and Bellevue Hospital at the same time. Mr. Rubildo received his undergraduate education from the University of New York State at Plattsburgh and attended New York University's graduate program.